CHELSEA HOUSE PUBLISHERS
New York • Philadelphia

CHELSEA HOUSE HEARTBEATS

This edition published 1994 by
Chelsea House Publishers, a division of Main Line Book Co.,
300 Park Avenue South, New York, N.Y. 10010
by arrangement with Heinemann

First published by Heinemann International
Literature and Textbooks in 1993

Cover illustration by Kevin Jones
Cover and text design by Threefold Design

ISBN 0-7910-2935-2

Phototypeset by
Cambridge Composing (UK) Ltd, Cambridge
Printed and bound in Great Britain
by Cox & Wyman Ltd, Reading, Berkshire

10 9 8 7 6 5 4 3 2 1

Contents

1

Desperate Girl

The vehicle's horn blared over the peaceful countryside, startling a young couple who were picking leaves from tea bushes. They paused in their work to look up the hill.

'Someone is being called,' guessed the boy.

'I wonder who, and why?' said the girl.

The horn blared again, giving two short blasts then a long one.

'Sounds urgent,' said the boy, removing the large basket from his back. 'I'd better go and check.'

'Wait!' said the girl. She took off her basket and was just setting it down when a female shape appeared on top of the hill, outlined against the sky, waving an arm. 'I think I'm wanted.' Hastily she removed her dirty apron and head-cloth, and patted her plaited hair. 'Just when I'm in such a mess!'

'Women!' the boy, Njao, who was her brother, said in mock disgust. 'Surely tea picking is not a fashion show, Waithera?'

Ignoring the remark, Waithera hurried through the waist-high tea bushes towards the road above. She was slightly anxious, for why would the lady who stood up there on the hill above come calling for her at such a time and in such a way? Up the hill she climbed with the ease of the healthy country girl she was. Soon she was clear of the hundreds of dark green tea bushes and scrambling up a field with two cows in it. She did not slow down as the hill became steeper, and soon she joined her waiting friend.

Mama Asha was a well-groomed young woman in her early thirties. Well-patterned hair pieces framed her smooth, round features. She was wearing a softly-coloured, expensive two-piece dress. Her necklace and handbag were also good; but the finest thing about her was kindness. It was with genuine delight that the girl went to her and clasped her hand in both of hers.

'Mama Asha! What a . . . pleasant . . . surprise!' she exclaimed, panting after the exertion of hurrying up the hill. 'But you shouldn't . . . be standing by the road. Do come down to the house.'

'I don't want to bother your family at work, Waithera,' Asha's mother said in a gentle voice. 'I only wanted to see you, for I have both bad and good news for you.'

Waithera's bright face clouded with worry. 'Bad? Did you say bad?'

'I'll explain as we go along,' Mama Asha said, leading the girl away from the vehicle, a grey, corporation Land Rover with an aerial mast on top of the cab, and its driver. The two women strolled together for a while while the girl recovered her breath. Then they stopped, turned and looked at each other.

They were standing on high ground, and the country spread out like a map below them. The whole area was a fertile one, with a mass of green hills which looked blue in the distance. Not far to the west stretched a range of mountains, while in the distant north-east the great mountain with its sharp, snow-covered peaks reached for the sky. The morning sun shone from a blue sky which was clear of clouds except for those which always seemed to hug the mountains. Yet, in spite of the sun, it felt cool because of a steady breeze which ruffled their hair and made their skirts billow suddenly.

'What's happened?' Waithera asked anxiously. 'Asha isn't ill again, is she?'

'She's fine,' Mama Asha replied soothingly, and then paused, wondering which news she ought to give Waithera first. She studied the brown, oval face which did not need make-up to be pretty, and the healthy figure which was appealing even in the simple, striped dress.

A year earlier, Waithera had been taking leaves to the collection centre and had found the then six-year-old Asha crying by the roadside. The little girl had injured her foot by stepping on a nail on her way home from school. Waithera had given her first aid, and abandoned the leaves she'd picked to carry the child home. They'd been friends ever since. The little girl often went to see Waithera at the collection centre, waiting there until her mother came for her. Waithera's cheerful nature attracted Mama Asha as well, and the three of them often spent Sundays together.

Mama Asha had come to learn that Waithera was not the simple country girl she perhaps looked, but was very well educated. Like so many others, she had not been fortunate enough to get a job, but, unlike some, she was not too proud to soil her hands helping her parents on the farm.

'The bad news is that we're leaving,' Mama Asha began. 'We'll miss you terribly.'

'Whaat . . . ?' Waithera gasped, wide-eyed. 'Are you being transferred?'

'No. I'm resigning to go and manage an estate my husband has bought at the coast.'

'I'm glad for you,' Waithera said as a sense of deep loss gripped her, 'though I can't pretend I'm not disappointed. You'll be *hundreds* of kilometres away.'

'No more pleasant Sundays with them,' she added to herself, 'with outings, hair dressing, video shows and laughter.' Her face was sad.

'Cheer up! At least I want to leave you my job,' Mama Asha consoled the girl.

'No more playful visits from little Asha,' Waithera went on to herself, looking down, 'or presents from this wonderful mama.'

Suddenly she looked up, staring at her friend. 'Wait!

What did you say? Did I hear you say . . . say . . . or didn't I?'

Mama Asha smiled at her. 'Yes, dear. I said I have both bad and good news. The good news is that I want you to take over my job.'

Waithera was speechless. Mama Asha was the factory's leaf officer. She supervised all the collection centres and made sure the factory bought and processed good quality leaves. It was the kind of job Waithera had always dreamed of and prayed for.

'The idea occurred to me a short while ago after I'd given in my resignation. The boss seemed to have appreciated my work, for he said he was sorry to lose me. He asked me to choose a leaving gift from him. I had a hard time choosing, when it suddenly occurred to me that to have you take my place would be the best thing he could do for me. I didn't tell him so, for I had to see you first. You'd like it, wouldn't you?'

'Wouldn't I!' Waithera gasped dreamily. 'My education wouldn't be wasted, and I wouldn't be a burden on my parents any more.'

Waithera pointed down at a half-built house. 'Poor father; he stopped building to send me to college. But instead of helping him now I'm asking for more, just when he is desperately trying to send my brother to college as well, not to mention coping with Mother's diabetes.'

'I had all that in mind, Waithera, for you always think of others before yourself.'

Waithera was overcome with gratitude which made her eyes shine with tears. 'You're too good to me,' she said, hugging her friend. 'I don't know why, because I don't deserve it.'

'Don't thank me yet,' Mama Asha cautioned. 'There are two snags.'

This worried the girl. 'What snags?'

'First, the boss has to accept the idea, and it won't be easy. You're qualified, but you're young and inexperienced. However, he respects my judgement, and he won't want to disappoint me.'

'What's the second snag?' Waithera asked. Hope was fading.

Mama Asha studied the young face intently. 'I hope we won't have to face it,' she replied without going into details. 'We'll talk with the boss now. Come on.'

'Surely not in my condition?' Waithera protested, looking down at her old gardening dress.

'He won't see you,' Mama Asha laughed. Waithera followed her doubtfully to the Land Rover. Mama Asha told the driver to excuse them for a while, and they climbed into the cab and closed the doors. It was only when she picked up a microphone and contacted the factory by radio that Waithera understood.

'This is Mama Asha,' she began. 'Get me the boss, please.'

'Hang on for a moment,' said a clear, feminine voice from the speaker.

Two minutes later, a low but authoritative masculine voice came on. 'Well, Mama? Where did you disappear to?'

'To inspect a collection centre, sir,' Mama Asha lied. 'I've been thinking over the present you promised.'

'Oh, good,' said the voice. 'Worth fifty pounds, I hope.'

'I don't want money.' Mama Asha hesitated. 'I would like you to replace me with a friend of mine instead.'

The voice broke into laughter. 'I'll make it worth eighty pounds.'

The women glanced at each other uneasily. 'If you please, sir, considering my friend would please me more than eighty pounds would.'

'Final offer: a hundred pounds!'

Mama Asha turned the microphone off and told the downcast Waithera to wait outside, but the girl did not move. She turned the mike on again and continued, 'Please do me this one, final favour, sir.'

'Dear Mama Asha,' the low, curt voice answered a little more gently, 'we can't let personal favours influence appointments. It's one of the factors contributing to the collapse of many public corporations.'

'You know me; I wouldn't recommend anyone who wasn't qualified.'

'Any experience?'

'Brought up in this tea zone and deeply interested.'

'Oh, well,' the voice said in resignation, 'tell the fellow to call on me at nine tomorrow morning. I won't promise anything, but I'll grant a fair interview. Continue working in the meantime. I'm not releasing you until the end of the week. Over and out.'

'How disgusting!' Mama Asha exclaimed, replacing the microphone. 'He actually expects a man!'

'Do you think it's wise for me to see him?' Waithera asked nervously.

'But of course! You'll have to face the beast in the morning and hope for the best.'

2

Heartless Beast?

Waithera was at the factory gate next morning, where her friend was waiting for her. The sun was just rising in the east, and the morning was bright, but Waithera was uneasy.

'You told me to dress like a responsible person,' she told Mama Asha. 'Am I all right?'

Mama Asha studied her friend critically. Waithera's soft hair was neatly combed back and held with a pretty pin at the back. Her long-sleeved blouse was a spotless white. With it she wore a short, sleeveless coat and pleated skirt, both a sky blue colour. Her light shoes were black.

'You'll do,' Mama Asha approved. But she felt uneasy as she looked at the clear, light-skinned face before her, though the gate-keeper was gazing at it in admiration. She did not tell Waithera why, but continued, 'You must try to appear sure of yourself.'

'I don't feel it. Tell me, Mama Asha – is the big man terribly – er – overwhelming?'

The lady smiled. 'You mean is Mwea formidable? You'll have to find out for yourself. However, I can promise you he won't eat you up!'

But Waithera was not reassured as they walked towards the offices. The factory was built on sloping ground. As well as the office block there were stores, garages and two huge buildings full of humming machines which were belching out smoke into the sky. Parked around the area were many leaf collection lorries, a few tractors and some smaller vehicles. People were busy but at this hour the vehicles were not. Below the factory area were well-built dwelling houses. Farther down the valley was a river and a water plant.

Mama Asha pointed at the main office and a white Pajero.

'Go now. He is in if you see that car. Sorry I can't take you in – those field clerks over there have to be briefed. See me after you're through.'

Waithera pulled herself together and went into a spacious office which seemed to be more full of filing cabinets than clerks. A short, thickset, round-headed man in an expensive suit stopped giving instructions as she entered.

He certainly looked formidable! Waithera thought nervously.

However, the man's dark face lit up with interest at the sight of her. He came over and his voice was as friendly as his face as he welcomed her. 'Make yourself at home. Come right in. Come! Please take a seat.

Waithera went forward and sat down as the man sat opposite her. 'Tell me what we can do for you.'

'I – I came for . . .' she began, when it suddenly occurred to her that the man in front of her was not the one she had heard on the radio. This voice was far too jolly, for one thing. 'I mean I want to see the manager.'

'Is he expecting you?'

'Yes, he is.'

The man gestured to a side door. 'Go ahead.'

Nervous again, Waithera went to the door and knocked on it.

'Come in,' said the low, curt voice she had heard over the radio.

She stood gazing at the man with her mouth slightly open, for he was not what she had expected. She was looking at a man in his early thirties, a bit taller than average and dressed simply but neatly in a dark brown shirt and trousers which fitted his fine, athletic figure to perfection. His appearance suggested he would have been more at home in the field than in an office. He had a quiet, calm look about him but his eyes were sharp and alert. He had been standing by the window studying some papers. Now he looked up and stood gazing back at the girl in silence.

Not formidable, Waithera decided, but rather nice. But the way his keen eyes were watching her made her uncomfortable. It was hard to tell from his face whether he was interested or just curious. She forced herself not to lower her own gaze and smiled. 'Good morning,' she said as confidently as she could.

'Good morning,' he replied. 'Can I help you?'

'Yes, please.'

'Close the door.'

She did, but unlike the man in the outer office, this one, Mr Mwea, did not invite her to sit down. He went on studying her. 'We haven't met, or I'd remember,' he commented.

'I believe I've seen you drive past a few times, but we haven't met formally.'

'To what, then, do I owe the privilege of meeting you?'

'I've come for an interview. You said – I mean Mama Asha told me you had agreed to give me one this morning.'

Mwea raised his eyebrows, which was probably his way of expressing surprise. 'I was expecting a man, or at least a more mature mama.'

'I'm not all that young.'

'Too young and charming,' he muttered.

'Please don't be prejudiced, sir. You said – I was told you'd grant me a fair interview.'

He paused to think, trying to remember what he'd said to Mama Asha. 'So I did,' he said, sounding resigned. 'Oh, well, perhaps we could use you in something else.' He held out his hand. 'Your credentials, please.'

She produced the documents from her handbag and gave them to him. Putting aside his own papers, he leaned against a filing cabinet and studied them. The ID card revealed she was Emma Waithera Wagema, born in that location. He was surprised to learn she was twenty-four because she looked twenty. Her school certificate showed she had attended a national secondary school and passed with second division. He noted she had done English and Science subjects well. But what he studied for long time was the diploma in Agriculture from a leading college of Agriculture, Science and Technology. She had done advanced Botany and Bacteriology, among other things.

He turned from the document in his hand and studied her more closely. She was encouraged to see him smile and say, 'Sit down, Miss Wagema.'

'Thank you.'

He also sat down, behind his executive desk, facing her, leaning back in a relaxed way. 'Your testimonials are fine, but I take it you have no previous experience.'

The word 'experience' irritated Waithera like many other jobseekers, for every employer was after the same thing. 'Experience has to start somewhere,' she replied without pausing to frame her words in a better way. 'Where will experience come from in the future if managers don't encourage new talent?'

He reluctantly admitted to himself she had a point. 'Do you know what the job is all about?' he asked.

'A bit. Inspecting all the leaf collection centres. Determining leaf quality before processing.'

He nodded. 'What's remarkable about this factory?'

'It pays the best prices to the farmers in the district.' She had heard her father say that.

'Why?'

'Because of leaf quality.'

He nodded again. 'Now perhaps you understand the responsibility of this post. We can't give it to just anyone. Tell me now, Miss Wagema – how would you go about it?'

Waithera paused to think this time. 'I'd aim for even higher quality. From the source. I'd keep taking soil samples and have the farmers advised accordingly. I'd ask the administration to organise meetings about this, and request the factory to be more generous in providing material for tending the crop.'

It encouraged her more to see him smile again, and she began to relax as well.

'Which are our major foreign exchange earners? Which is declining and why?'

'Tourism, coffee and tea industries. Coffee is declining, perhaps because of poor prices, management and farming.'

'I'd hate tea to face the same fate. Now name three of our best customers.'

She could only remember two. 'Britain and Pakistan.'

'Where did tea drinking begin?'

'India? China? Japan?' she replied uncertainly. 'I mean somewhere in Asia?'

'Never mind.' He wrote down the word *coup*. 'Pronounce this.'

She wondered if he was testing her general knowledge or amusing himself. But he was not amused when she got it wrong by pronouncing it 'kuup'.

He picked up the phone and issued brief instructions in a low voice. Presently a young man brought in a tray with several green leaves on it, then left. Each stalk had two tender leaves and a bud. 'Separate the good quality leaves from the poor.'

Waithera knew this was the crucial part of the interview. She used her training and experience at the farm to separate the leaves carefully. He lit a cigarette and sat watching the girl more than what she was doing. He noticed her hands were rough from work, unlike her face which was so soft and smooth. Soon she was finished and he saw that, apart from separating the two grades, she had put a few pairs of leaves aside.

'What are those?' he asked.

'Rejects.'

'Why?' he asked, since some of them looked all right to him.

'This one has no bud as you can see. The other three are so poor they are unfit.'

'I see,' he said, though he did not, since he was not a botanist like her. He hesitated, pulled a drawer open, took out some forms and gave them to her. 'Fill these in.'

Her eyes and face lit up in wonderment. 'You – you mean I get the job?'

'No. It means you'll be considered.'

She lowered her eyes in embarrassment and started filling in the application forms. He picked up the papers he had been reading and studied them as she wrote. But she had a feeling he was actually watching her all the time. Half way through she couldn't bear it any longer, and she looked up to catch him staring at her in a manner which could not be misunderstood. She was used to being admired, but this man's eyes were more intense. And he was so – well, masculine. She found herself staring back against her will. She trembled, and her pen fell on the floor, breaking the momentary spell. She picked it up and went on filling in the forms, making several errors. He noticed this and went to the window with his papers. He did not look at her again until she had finished.

'Do you need this job much?' he asked gently, towering over her as he took the forms.

'Very, very much.'

'Why?'

'Firstly because of family problems. Secondly because I'd enjoy it.'

'Where do you live?'

'With my parents, five kilometres down the main road.'

'Look at me and listen, Waithera.'

She looked up slowly, once more aware of his intense gaze. His breath hissed through his clenched teeth as he stared down at the angelic face with its pure eyes with dark pupils, small nose and slightly open, purple lips. 'I'd like to know you better. I want you to wait for me by the road at your place at six. We could drive somewhere for dinner, then we'll see if you can get the job, and a personal loan to help you get started.'

'Please!' gasped a startled Waithera, rising to her feet.

Her plea fell on deaf ears. 'Six o'clock,' he repeated, leading her to the door before she could protest. 'I think that's all for the present. See you later.'

Waithera walked out like someone in a daze, leaving the clerks in the outer office staring after her. She hurried towards the gate. But as she walked out of the factory she heard someone running and calling after her. It was Mama Asha. Waithera waited for her.

'I saw you leave. Why didn't you stop to tell me what happened?'

'I'm sorry. I'm so confused. I . . .'

Mama Asha noticed how disturbed Waithera was. 'Did you fail the interview?'

'I don't think so. He gave me forms to fill in. But . . .'

'But what?'

'I'd rather not talk about it.'

Mama Asha was disturbed as well. 'Then it's as I feared! You've met the second snag!'

'So you *knew* when you talked of another snag yesterday!'

'Yes, dear, I feared it, for I know him. The problem with you is that you're too pretty. That's why I told you to dress formally. But you're lovely without even trying. I did hope he wouldn't fancy you – he usually prefers the more sophisticated type – but I should have known better.'

They started walking up the drive towards the main road.

'Poor, lucky you!' Mama Asha commented suddenly.

'What do you mean?'

'You'll know heaven and hell.'

'I'll know nothing of the kind,' Waithera retorted, 'because I'll have nothing to do with him.'

'You'd know you have little choice in the matter, if only you knew as much about him as I do.'

Waithera stopped. 'What kind of man is he?'

'It's not good to talk ill of your boss, especially when he has been nice to someone as he has been to me, but you're my friend and I introduced you to him, so I should warn you. He's quite manly, as you saw. He is also active, sharp and forceful in business. Socially he is well up, amusing and generous. But in love he is heartless. "Love 'em and leave 'em" seems to be his motto.'

'Quite a womaniser?'

'Not much, but once in a while he ensnares a girl, shows her the good life and then discards her.'

They moved on and Waithera digested this information gloomily. 'I can't go out with someone I don't know; someone trying to take advantage of my situation.'

'I don't know why he's acted that way,' Mama Asha said. 'He's never seduced any of his workers.'

'Well, I think he's contemptible!' Waithera declared vehemently.

They reached the main road and stood waiting.

'I'm very sorry this happened, Waithera.'

'Don't worry. I'll be all right. But oh! Mama Asha, I don't want to throw away this chance, and he is coming at six. What should I do?'

'Search me. I can't advise you to throw away such an opportunity, or your principles, either. I know what most girls would do, but do what you think is best.'

A colourful minibus came roaring round a bend and pulled up before them. Waithera said goodbye to her friend and boarded it. She thought over her dilemma as the bus roared down the road.

At a few minutes to six, a white Pajero with a couple of slim orange and blue stripes down the sides hummed down the same road. The gentleman, Mwea, behind the wheel had a faraway look, and he was smiling faintly to himself. He managed to keep to his own lane, but he was not aware of much, not even the way the sky above the wall of mountains in the west was turning to a blaze of gold.

In fact, he had not managed to concentrate on anything all day. All he could think of was a vision of beauty and innocence itself, in the form of a simple girl, staring up at him with wide, pure eyes. He was annoyed with himself for looking at his watch every now and then, waiting for the hour. Time seemed to drag its heels. At last the hour had come, and he had slipped on his jacket. Now here he was, going to meet her.

She seemed inexperienced, and it would be fun to awaken her, he thought. At the back of his mind, however, was the nagging fear that she would not be there. He realised he had handled her a bit crudely.

'She'd better be there if she knows what's good for her!' Mwea said to himself grimly.

Four kilometres down the road he slowed down and started looking for her. People were going home after delivering leaves or shopping. Occasionally he came across a young couple talking by the roadside, but the girl he wanted was not there. He looked at the mileage indicator and was annoyed to find he had still not seen her even five kilometres further on. There was a village woman standing by a basket of leaves farther down the road. She was dressed typically with a patterned sheet wrapped round the lower part of her body, over an old dress. She was also wearing a headcloth. As he slowed down she became alert.

'How are you, Mama?' he greeted her in the vernacular. 'Have you seen one Emma Waithera around here?'

She came forward, smiling sadly. 'Don't you recognise me, sir?' she asked in good English.

Her words made him start, though he was not easily shocked. He stared and saw that even if the neat hair was covered by the headcloth and the healthy curves were hidden by the old dress and sheet, there was no mistaking the lovely face.

'I – I had to help my brother pick tea because Mother is sick and Father is away,' she said softly. 'But I'm not making any excuses.'

He was not listening to her fully. Snubbed! he thought, sick with dismay. By a peasant!

'I waited for you to thank you for the interview,' she went on quietly, looking down at her hands, 'but I can't come out this evening. I'd hate to annoy you by being unco-operative in certain matters.'

'Don't tell me nobody has ever made a pass at you!' he snapped, making her wince.

'I may be desperate, but at least I hope I'll always have some self respect,' she replied quietly, moving back to pick up the large basket of leaves, which she hung from her head. 'I have to deliver these; I'm late.' She smiled that sad smile again. 'I suppose it's no use my asking if my application is accepted or not, is there?'

'We'll be in touch!' he replied furiously, and drove off in the same manner.

3

Back from the Past

'What is the matter with you, Waithera?' her mother asked two days later. Waithera had been very quiet since the day before, which was unlike her.

They were resting in the shade of a tree near their incomplete house. The mother was seated on a stool, sorting bad beans from the good for lunch.

Waithera looked up from the book she was reading and smiled in an unconvincing manner. 'I am all right.'

She had not told her family about the interview, to avoid disappointing them, as had happened twice before. It seemed one could get nowhere without bribery, or someone influential to arrange things. Well, Mama Asha had paved the way for her and she had spoiled it. She did not regret her decision, but she mourned the loss of what might have been. She had not heard from the factory and she was not surprised. After what she'd done it was unlikely Mr Mwea would even bother to write a letter of regret. 'We'll contact you' meant 'Forget it'. Her application forms were probably in the waste basket.

Suddenly Waithera became alert. She could hear the sound of a motor vehicle coming downhill towards the house. She jumped up and hurried to the gate. It was Mama Asha and her driver in their Land Rover.

Waithera was pleased. They had not seen one another since the interview. Mama Asha probably wanted to know what had happened between herself and Mr Mwea, thought Waithera unhappily. She did not want to remember what had taken place.

She opened the rough gate in welcome. The vehicle drove in and Mama Asha got out. She was wearing a flowery *kitenge* dress. She chatted with her young friend while the driver parked the vehicle. Then she was led into the house and introduced to Waithera's parents.

'Did you decide to meet the boss last evening but one?' Mama Asha asked finally, just as Waithera had feared.

'Yes,' she answered uncomfortably, 'but only to say no. I'm afraid I wasn't polite. I'd changed into my gardening dress, and was taking leaves to the collection centre.'

'You should have been more tactful,' Mama Asha said disapprovingly before opening her handbag and producing a letter. 'He sent me to deliver this.'

'He did?' a puzzled Waithera asked, taking the letter. 'What did he tell you?'

'Nothing. He just told me to deliver it and report back.'

Waithera looked at the letter uneasily. The medium-sized envelope was neatly addressed. Obviously a regret, together with the copies of her certificates. She took a deep breath and opened it.

Dear Miss Wagema, it began. *I am pleased to inform you that your application to join our corporation as Senior Leaf Officer has been successful. Your appointment is effective from tomorrow, subject to confirmation from headquarters. Efficiency and dedication is what is expected of you. Kindly sign the enclosed contract and return the same by the bearer. I wish you the best of luck in your new duties. Yours faithfully, J. N. Mwea, General Manager.*

Waithera's heart was pounding in wonder and disbelief. As the full meaning of the letter sunk in, her face lit up in sheer joy. '*Ee-yu-hu*!' she shouted, and began to dance.

'You mean he's offered you the job?' Mama Asha exclaimed, rising to her feet to share her friend's joy.

Waithera flung her arms around her friend and hugged her. 'Yes, Mama Asha dear. Thank you very much!'

She rushed out to her parents. 'I'm taking over Mama Asha's job!' she blurted out. 'I am the new senior leaf inspector!'

'Are you serious?' gasped her mother.

'Yes, Mammi.'

'God be praised,' she said, looking heavenward with raised hands.

'I knew all the time that my daughter was made for great things,' said her father, spitting on his chest in the traditional way of thanksgiving. 'That is why I invested heavily in her education.'

'I won't disappoint you, Father. I'll share your burdens.'

'In the meantime, you will need something to get started.' He turned to Waithera's mother. 'What are you waiting for, woman? Rush to the bank and clear out our account. See if we can afford a dress and shoes. I won't have my daughter going around in rags. Tell your son to kill the cock for supper. I shall need a hundred or two shillings to drink with my fellow *wazee*. They are going to realise tonight that I am Wagema, father of Waithera. From now onward, they are going to keep quiet when I cough, for none of them will sell leaves without my daughter's approval!'

Waithera laughed. When she did something wrong, she was her mother's daughter; when she did it right, she was *his* daughter. She left him bragging and returned to her guest.

They took cocoa (which they preferred to tea!) as they read the contract. Waithera noted the salary was not as high as she'd expected, but there was overtime, a free house and transport.

'You'll have to move into my house as soon as I leave,' Mama Asha said. 'We operate twenty-four hours a day, you know.'

'Not until I can afford furniture.'

They paused to look at each other. It was Waithera who said what they were both thinking: 'I wonder why he accepted me after all.'

Mama Asha went on looking at her. 'Whatever his failings, I don't think he'd let personal things influence his judgement, if he thought you were suitable for the post. And yet . . .'

'And yet what?' Waithera said eagerly, leaning forward.

'Let's wait and see.'

'The first thing is for you to report to the boss,' Mama Asha told her friend the next morning.

'Just as I feared,' Waithera answered nervously. 'Can't you come with me this time?'

'I shall. As a matter of fact, he told me to bring you. But for goodness' sake! Be more confident. I shan't be around much longer.'

The girl did not feel confident, though she was dressed a little more boldly. 'How did he react after you returned the forms yesterday?' she asked as they walked towards the offices.

'It's hard to tell with him, but I could have sworn he was relieved – as if he thought you'd refuse. He asked me a few questions about you and your family, and I told him what I could.'

'What kind of questions?'

'General.'

They reached the offices. The white Pajero was outside. 'He arrives early?' asked Waithera.

'Very, but he also leaves early. I believe he has property somewhere else.'

Mama Asha greeted those in the outer office and knocked on the door of the inner one.

'Come in,' the low voice called.

'Good morning, Mr Mwea,' Mama Asha greeted him cheerfully.

'Morning, Asha,' he replied with a lazy smile, which flickered out as his eyes rested on Waithera. Her lovely features were crowned with soft curls. The black dress showed off her healthy curves, shapely legs and light brown complexion. Over the square collar lay flame coloured beads and hugging the slim waist was a broad belt.

'G-Good morning, sir,' Waithera stammered.

Mwea had unconsciously held his breath. He let it out and smiled casually again. 'Good morning, Miss Wagema. Do sit down, both of you.'

They sat down, facing him. He put aside some papers and relaxed, leaning back in his chair, resting the back of his head on his hands and stretching his legs. The women were aware of his lean, powerful muscles beneath the white shirt, and the quiet face with lively eyes.

'I'd like to welcome you to the factory, Miss Wagema.'

'Thank you.'

'You claimed you'd aim for even higher quality the other day,' he reminded her. 'I'll expect you to bear it in mind as you undertake your new duties.'

'I shall.'

'Feel free to consult me in case of difficulties, and please consider yourself among friends.'

He turned to Mama Asha. 'I expect you to teach her as much as possible before you go. Show her around the factory and collection centres. Let her meet the field clerks she'll be supervising. Don't forget the farms; starting from the lower zone to the highest. I want a comprehensive report. I think that's all.'

Waithera spent the rest of the day at the factory, meeting the rest of the staff, seeing the office and the manufacturing plant itself where she saw how the leaves were withered, fermented, dried, ground, tasted and packed.

On the second day they visited seven collection centres of the lower, warmer zone in the Land Rover. Waithera was not happy with the quality; much work was needed. On the third day they went round the middle zone; this was better. On the fourth day they were to go to the remote, high zone.

After welcoming her on the first day, Mr Mwea seemed to have lost interest in her; in fact, she rarely saw him. He worked for a few hours a day and then drove off, to reappear shortly after sunrise the following day. At the back of her mind she had been afraid of another awkward moment with him, but it seemed her fears were not justified.

The two friends were in the remote high zone near the mountain, at one of the collection centres. The centre was just a long shed where people spread out their leaves to be inspected before putting them in basket-like bags, to be hung on lorries later. After checking the leaves and cautioning the two clerks there, they rested outside. Below was a flat, green valley. Opposite was the tree-covered mountain. They could see a couple of brown elephants moving slowly through the forest. The wind was chilly in spite of the afternoon sun. A few clouds hung beneath the mountain peaks.

They turned from the mountain at the sound of an approaching motor vehicle. Waithera was surprised to see Mwea's white Pajero. It came to a halt near their Land Rover. They went over to it, since he did not alight.

'Afternoon, ladies. How is this centre?'

'It has both quality and quantity,' Mama Asha replied. 'But we had to caution the clerks for overlooking many unsuitable leaves.'

'Be strict. What about the report?'

'I'm still compiling it,' said Waithera, patting a file she was holding. 'It will be ready by tomorrow.'

He nodded and turned to Mama Asha. 'Go back to the factory and dismiss the driver for the rest of the day.' He opened the passenger door. 'As for you, Miss Wagema, get in; I want to talk to you.'

Waithera's heart leapt. She directed an appealing look at Mama Asha, who just shrugged helplessly. Her heart beating, the girl entered the spacious vehicle and sat on the comfortable passenger seat. Mwea drove down the winding, earthen road to the green valley below and on to the very edge of the forest, where he stopped the vehicle.

He produced fishing gear from the boot and led Waithera to a small river whose sparkling waters ran over gentle falls and smooth rocks. On their side there was green grass while the opposite bank had a background of bushes with wild flowers of various colours. The only sounds in the air were those of the waterfalls and chirping birds. Mwea sat on a grey boulder at the edge of the river and cast his hook into the clear water.

'I come here occasionally when I want peace and quiet,' he explained. 'And you, my dear, are going to stop looking at me with suspicion. Sit down beside me and feel at peace with the world.'

She sat reluctantly on the boulder near him. She looked at the wonders of nature around her, but was more conscious of the man beside her. She stole sidelong glances at him. The rather long hair ran down the sides of his otherwise clean-shaven face. That face was more relaxed today; even the sharp eyes were, making him almost good looking. His white shirtsleeves were folded back, baring strong, dark brown arms. Brown terylene trousers and casual white shoes completed the picture of a pleasant, ordinary fellow. It was a pity he had a bad reputation.

He was also very conscious of her presence, though he pretended to concentrate on the fishing. He resisted an urge to keep his eyes on her, and had to be content with her image on the clear water, which was often spoiled by ripples. She was lovelier than ever with the smooth, shiny curls over the clear, brown features. The blue silk dress with puffed up short sleeves and low neckline was tight at the top and pleated at the bottom showing off the firm breasts and slim waist more than ever. Her necklace, broad black belt with a bronze butterfly, and gleaming black shoes completed her dazzling appearance.

She was suddenly conscious that he was watching her, and she returned his look through the water. He grinned at her; she smiled back before turning away. She only looked at him again when he got a bite and she watched him wind up the line and pull out a struggling fish. He caught another twenty minutes later. She relaxed like him since it appeared he did not want to talk after all.

'Bored?' he asked at last.

'Not at all,' she smiled. 'Resting during working hours with the permission of the boss suits me perefctly!'

'Forget the "boss" business. I brought you here in my personal capacity, for I'd like us to know one another better. Let's tell each other our life stories; our likes and dislikes; our fears and hopes.'

'Shh! You'll scare the fish away!'

'They can swim to the ocean for all I care! I was going to tell you I have more than a passing interest in you.'

'After the way I treated you?'

'Especially.' He paused. 'Let me explain: eight years ago, when I was a junior officer, I fell in love with a girl as lovely as yourself. So much that I wanted to marry her. She thought I had a promising career and she agreed. But on the day I was to take her to see my parents, she went to spend the weekend at the coast with someone who was wealthier than I. My heart broke; so much I've never recovered fully.

'Since then, I've believed that the only thing women love is money. So I made it, and I used it to get a few other girls. But as our relationship was purely commercial, none of the affairs lasted long.

'I'm telling you this to try to make you understand why I tried to make a date with you the first time I saw you. I thought all I had to do was dangle the job and a "loan" and you'd give in. But when I found I was wrong, I was ashamed of myself.'

Waithera was startled by his confession, and she dreaded hearing what he was driving at.

'Now do you see why I acted towards you the way I did?'

'Yes, but . . .' She did not add how she could not quite see how one loose, greedy girl could make a man hold the rest in contempt. Anyhow, she did not want to understand; she had been forewarned about him. She would not be another of his victims. She would resist his advances by all the means at her disposal.

He sensed her doubts. 'If only you knew how I felt, perhaps you'd understand. For the present I only ask you to forgive me if I offended you.'

'I do,' she murmured, 'just as I hope you forgive me for meeting you dressed the way I was. I – I didn't mean to offend you. I thought you'd turn down my application, and I had no choice but to go on picking tea. But you offered me the job after all, so I was mistaken about you.'

'Just as I was mistaken about you, so let's say we're quits. Now hold this,' he added, giving her the fishing gear. 'If you feel a fish tugging at the end of the line, pull it out the way I did.'

He went to the car and returned with wrapped-up roast beef, fruits and sodas. He was surprised to find she had caught a fish as well. She was on her feet, yelling as she struggled with it. He laughed as she pulled it out in a violent, clumsy manner.

'Well, well! not bad for a beginner,' he commented.

'You're jealous!' she cried in excitement. 'It's bigger than both of yours!'

She was completely at ease with him as they ate the picnic, talking light-heartedly, and he had a taste of her cheerful nature for the first time. He was about to light a cigarette when a drop of rain fell on his forehead.

They got to the vehicle just as the rain came down. It got heavier and heavier and the lightning flashed and thunder crashed over them. 'Driving out of here will be a nightmare,' he said.

The rain fell on and on. They sat talking until Waithera got worried about darkness approaching. Mwea started the Pajero and drove it slowly out of the valley. He engaged the four-wheel drive as the car started swaying and twisting up the wet, earthen road, its wipers trying to cope with the downpour. The headlights shone into the pouring rain. Since the driver and the vehicle were reliable, the girl did not find the drive frightening. It took nearly an hour to cover the ten kilometres to the main tarmac road. Then they drove more quickly to the lower zone, where there was no rain, only moonlight. They drove past the factory, to stop further down, by Waithera's farm.

'Thank you very much for the half day off!' she said cheerfully, picking up her file and getting out.

'Aren't you taking your fish?'

'That's all right; Mother'll have made supper.'

He got out as well and escorted her a little way down the steep drive to her house. She held out her hand. 'Good night, and thanks for everything again.'

He took her hand. 'Good night, Waithera. Would you like to go somewhere a bit more lively sometime?'

'Yes, please!' she said impulsively, her bright face beaming and her eyes glinting in the moonlight.

He stared at the face, swore and took her roughly in his strong arms. 'You're too much; you angel!'

He pressed her against him. Her beauty and fragrance filled him, and he felt a sweet tremor shake him to the core of his being. He felt her shudder and he put his arms round her slim waist. He lowered his lips to seek out hers, but she turned her face away.

'No! No! Never!' she protested. She struggled, weakly at first and then fiercely.

He reluctantly let go of her.

'On second thoughts, I shall never, never go anywhere with you again!' she said, panting, before disappearing into the darkness.

He was left cooling down and cursing himself for handling her the wrong way for the second time. He was rushing her like an amateur. It seemed she had enchanted him so much that he had lost his senses.

'But I shall never, never give up until you surrender,' he promised himself.

4

The Beauty Spot

Mwea wondered what Waithera's attitude towards him would be after the rough way he had treated her. He did not find out because he did not see her at all the following day. Only Mama Asha came to his office at around noon.

'A week has passed,' she reminded him. 'I must start getting ready to leave, please, Mr Mwea. My husband is coming for me on Saturday.'

'Why the hurry?' he asked, gesturing at her to sit opposite him. 'Have you finished handing over?'

'Quite. My work is now in good hands.'

'Where is Waithera?' he asked.

'She has been compiling the report at the office since eight. She's just handed it to your secretary for typing and left for the field.'

Avoiding me, he thought uneasily. 'What was her mood?' he asked aloud.

'Restless,' Mama Asha told him accusingly. 'You know, I've gone through her analysis of the crop and recommendations for improvement. It all made a lot of sense to me. I should have done the same when I first came here. It would be too bad if circumstances prevented her from completing the task.'

'What makes you say that?' he asked sharply.

'I'm just quoting Waithera.'

She was more upset than he suspected, he thought, and cursed himself.

'Pardon me if you think me nosy,' Mama Asha said, looking at him directly, 'but I brought this girl to you, and I have a personal interest in her. Tell me truthfully what your intentions are towards her.'

Mwea leaned back in his chair, his eyes half closed, searching his mind and heart. He had lain awake at night pondering over the same question; he had not lost sleep over a woman for many years.

He admitted to himself that when he'd first seen her in his office, he had merely lusted after her. If he'd had his way he'd have seduced her and paid her off. But after she had turned down his offer he had come to regard her in a new light. Funny how her sad smile as she carried her basket of leaves had haunted him. So had her words: 'I may be desperate, but at least I hope I'll always have self respect.'

He had learned more about her since then. It seemed she had many of the qualities he wanted in a woman; she was respectable, educated and hard working. She was also cheerful and affectionate. That she was lovely into the bargain was an added bonus. Decency, ability to take care of a home and the soil are of more importance to African men.

What of the sweet, electrifying feeling of having her in his arms? Somehow *that* overshadowed the more reasonable virtues!

He opened his eyes and answered Mama Asha. 'I want to love and cherish her forever, if she is what she seems.'

'*If?*' Mama Asha was disturbed. 'Please don't bother her if you have doubts. I told you her other problems.'

'You asked me to speak truthfully. My intentions are sincere. But you must understand I've been mistaken in a woman before. I've got to be cautious.'

'She *is* a good girl.' Mama Asha paused, leaned forward and added, 'You know, I like you, Mr Mwea. You're hard working but you're not getting any younger. It's high time you settled down. Waithera is just the type to make you do that, and you're just the kind of reliable man she deserves – if only you can be trusted.'

'I can be this time, believe me. What is the best way to win her affection?'

'Sincerity.'

'Anything else?'

'I can only advise you to be more careful. She can be pretty stubborn.'

'Thanks for telling me. Collect your dues tomorrow. We could hold a small party for you on Saturday.'

'That would be marvellous! It would be even more marvellous if you'd provide a lorry to carry my goods.'

'Of course,' he said. 'Tell Waithera to move in immediately after you leave the house.'

'She said she can't move in yet. Her father can only afford a few things.'

He thought over this. 'You know she has to be around late because the leaves keep on arriving at night. I want you to arrange to have the house renovated and furnished. I'll take care of the bill. Don't worry about the cost too much. Just get whatever you, as her friend, know would please her. But I warn you, she must not know I'm paying, or she might refuse. Let her think it's corporation property.'

Mama Asha stared at him in wonder. 'You mean you want to help her without her realising it? I'm beginning to believe you're sincere. It is a step forward in the right direction.'

Njambi looked at herself in the wardrobe mirror and worried over her future. Once her dark features had been flawless; now age and harsh living were catching up with them. If only Otieno had not smashed her cheek with his fist . . . He'd caught her entertaining another man when he was the one paying her rent. She'd had to stay indoors for over two months now, and was behind with all his bills. Above all she had to think of her child's future. Perhaps she could marry a nice stable man and let him worry about her problems.

The problem was to find a suitable man. Not that she'd had a shortage of them, but one by one they'd left her.

'The best man for me is my first boyfriend,' she decided. 'He was the only one who truly loved me and wanted to marry me; the one I loved most.' But he'd been unable to offer her much, and she had given in to the temptation of the minister's son – and he'd found out and broken their relationship. She still had an informant at the factory and knew he was now quite wealthy.

Njambi pulled a drawer open and produced a photo album. She opened it and studied the picture of a gentle looking young man with long hair and intelligent eyes. Tears glistened in her own eyes as she studied it.

'Perhaps the damage can still be mended. He is still single; I'm still quite good looking. What's more, I have something to offer him which cannot be denied. Perhaps I can get him to forgive me.'

It would be humiliating to seek him after all these years, but she had no choice. She would use all her charm and cunning.

Waithera did not try to avoid her boss for a second day, since she knew she could not do so for long. She had to meet him now and then in the course of her work. But she was determined, more than ever, not to be intimate with him.

She had come to this decision after analysing her feelings after he had hijacked her to the mountains. It was not that she had hated his company; on the contrary, she'd liked it. She'd even found herself responding to his passionate embrace – and that way lay danger.

She was tense when he summoned her to his office. However, he only wanted to discuss business in a friendly way. He told her he'd read her report and liked it. He'd forward her recommendations to the committee for approval.

She spent the rest of the day helping Mama Asha pack and prepare for her farewell party, which took place on Saturday evening. There was plenty of food, drinks and music, but no dancing. Mwea continued to treat Waithera in just a friendly way, but she noticed, like everybody else, that he had her seated at the main table with him, beside Mama Asha and her husband. She did not know it was a signal to all the hungry foxes in the factory to keep off her.

The following day was one of the saddest Sundays of her life, when she had to part with Asha and her mother. She was downcast for days, until the boss' secreatry called on her in her office with a bunch of keys. 'Your house is ready, Miss Wagema,' she said.

'Thank you.' Waithera understood Mama Asha had left the keys with the secretary to have it renovated. 'But I won't occupy it yet.'

'My instructions are that you're to move in immediately. Our leaf officer must be at hand at all times. I understand that is why it was furnished by the corporation. Mama Asha ordered some items and they've been delivered. You're to apply for a small advance if there's anything else you need.' She left quickly before the surprised Waithera could question her.

The girl closed the office quickly and went to the house, which was below the factory. Even the outside had been painted in cream and the flower garden had been tended. Waithera opened the front door and gasped.

It was a small but cosy two-bedroom affair. The walls were of pure cream cut with pink below. There was an elegant sofa suite with a coffee table, and a mahogany wall unit with a twenty-inch tele-video and radio cassette player with detachable speakers. In the bedroom was a divan bed and a wardrobe. The kitchen had new shelves, a cooker and fridge, while the bathroom had had a hot water system installed. It was surely a dream! She rolled on the big bed and gave a cry of delight: '*Ey-yu-hu*!'

These goods would have taken her a few years to save for,

but now she could afford things like utensils, bedding and curtains to make the house complete. Now she could concentrate on helping her family with her salary!

But later she began to wonder if the corporation usually bought furniture for its staff. Perhaps, but would it include electronic goods? She doubted it. All she was sure of was that she was being favoured, and she could guess on whose orders.

That cooled her excitement a bit. She wondered when he would come calling on her at night, expecting her to return the favour.

———— ♥ ————

Mwea did come eventually, but not at night. He came the following Saturday afternoon, his coat hung on his shoulder. He got a rude shock when he found her relaxed and laughing with a young man, complete with a 'box' hairstyle, jeans which were decorated with splashes of whitewash, and colourful casual shoes. They were having tea and home-baked cakes, and laughing over an American feature film on the tele-video screen.

Waithera stopped laughing and rose to her feet in embarrassment as he stood at the doorway. 'Mr Mwea! How nice! Do come in and join us for a cup of tea.'

He felt sick and furious to find she was a fast worker after all. It was just that she did not fancy old men like him. But he did not show his feelings as he declined her invitation. 'No thanks. I was just passing on my way home. I thought I'd glance in and see if you're comfortable. I see you are.'

His sarcasm did not escape her notice. She looked hurt for a moment, then she forced herself to smile and said, 'I insist you come in. There is someone here who has been eager to meet you.'

The young man came forward with a more sincere smile. 'She is right Mr Mwea. We are all eager to meet you. You can't imagine how grateful our parents are to you for fixing Waithera up.'

'It was nothing,' Mwea mumbled, utterly relieved and ashamed. A closer look at the young man revealed he was younger than Waithera, and though she was not dark like him, they resembled one another. Even their way of smiling was similar. Mwea did not need to be told he was her brother.

He sat down, and formal introductions were made over the tea. After one cup he said he had to leave, for he did not want people to gossip about her. This made Waithera realise she had perhaps wronged him by thinking he would come bothering her at night. It also reminded her she had been too busy avoiding and suspecting him to find time to express gratitude to him as her brother had done.

'A moment please,' she said and disappeared into the bedroom, leaving Mwea chatting to her brother.

Waithera reappeared, having tidied her hair, oiled her skin and changed into her black dress with a matching broad belt, over which was a white cardigan. Mwea was astonished. Was she offering to go out with him? Who said miracles could not happen?

He could still not believe his luck when she followed him to the car. 'Got an appointment somewhere?' he asked cautiously.

'Wouldn't you like to take me for a spin?' she asked shyly, looking at him sideways.

'You mean would I like to go to paradise?' he corrected her in his delight. 'Lady, I don't need a written invitation. Hop in!'

They drove up to the main road, then down, down to the lower zone, where they reached the highway. They headed north towards the largest mountain. Mwea pressed the gas pedal down and the white Pajero streaked across the countryside at high speed. Waithera wound up her window to shut out the screaming wind. On their left was the tea zone and on the right was the lower coffee growing one. Everywhere were green hills covered with crops and trees. Up and down the hills they sped, crossing rivers and passing shopping centres. Mwea was as enthusiastic as a boy.

'Slow down! I actually wanted us to talk.' Waithera had to shout to be heard because of the wind.

He reduced the speed to a mere forty. 'Then say something nice,' he urged. 'A single kind word from you would be worth my best collection of music.'

'Let's be serious, Mr – '

'Calling me "Mister" isn't kind for a start.'

'All right, Mwea. I want to know why you let Mama Asha order such expensive goods for me.'

'It was meant as an incentive for you to enjoy your work. Anyhow, you must realise you are a senior officer now, and I can't let you appear desperate for things to those under you.'

'That was very considerate of you. I want to express my heartfelt gratitude for all you've done for me so far. You mustn't think me ungrateful. I want us to be the best of friends at work and socially. As for er . . . love matters, please let them take their course. Please don't let's rush like we did the other night. I'm not all that experienced. I had a boy in high school and another in college, but that was the usual passing teenage stuff. I've never really been in love. When I do fall in love, it will be for life. I'll want it to be with someone I can trust.'

'I suppose you've made up your mind I'm not to be trusted?'

'I trust you,' she teased, giving him a sidelong look, 'as much as I'd trust a lamb with a leopard!'

'You're right,' he admitted. 'I don't even trust myself with you! I feel like hugging and kissing you every time I meet you. I'm amazed at my own restraint! It would serve you right, too, for bewitching me!'

'But how?' she asked innocently. 'I don't remember brewing a potion secretly for you to drink!'

'You don't need potions. A look from your eyes and a smile on your lips are far more potent.'

She laughed. 'If you're telling me this, I wonder what you tell *genuine* beauties!'

'I can't tell it to just anyone; it has to come from my innermost self. To me you're beauty incarnate. You're my paragon of womanhood.'

She liked the sound of that, though she did not fully understand him. 'Tell me again in simple language.'

'I mean to me you are beauty itself in the flesh. You are my idea of excellence in a woman.'

She had been taking his flattery lightly, but *that* touched her.

They drove on to a busy but unpolluted provincial town. Mwea guided the Pajero to a fine, four-storey building at the edge of the town. He put on his coat and they got out of the car.

He led her to a neat restaurant on the ground floor, and to a table near one of the large windows with lace curtains. Besides themselves there were a few other couples, four casually dressed European tourists, and a single lady sipping a drink at the other end.

'By the way, Waithera, my place is in that direction,' he said, pointing and looking through the window to a vast, flat zone which was bathed in pink by the setting sun.

'You go that far every day?'

'I have to. I am still developing it.'

He did not elaborate. They settled down to a meal and a bottle of mild wine. They talked light-heartedly, but most of the time they just looked at each other. Somehow he had made her lower her guard enough to make her look and smile back at him without feeling too shy.

Suddenly, Waithera felt someone else was watching her, and she turned her head. 'Does she have to stare at us so?'

'Who?' he asked, also turning.

'The lone lady in the corner.'

Mwea looked, then he became tense and stared hard at her.

'You know her?' asked Waithera.

Mwea did not answer. He continued to stare at her as if fascinated.

The lady rose to her feet and walked towards them slowly. Tall and slim, her curly hair was well groomed and she was wearing a dark woollen suit and high heels. Her movements were as graceful as her body, and she was smiling brightly.

Mwea's mind flashed back eight years. He had a momentary vision of a black beauty with flawless, rounded features; a laughing face with sparkling eyes and snow-white teeth; a lively face which had filled his days with so much joy. She had been everything to him and he had been obsessed with her, so much so that nothing short of marriage would have done.

The image changed to one of himself, tossing and weeping alone in bed, having nightmares of her getting into a white Mercedes sports, to go and make love to another man. She had hurt his pride to such an extent that he had lost all faith in women – and life itself.

His mind flashed back to the present. It was indeed true that time heals all wounds. He had sworn he would never see her again as long as he lived. Now he found he could face her without much bitterness or regret, especially when he had someone as sweet as Waithera beside him.

'Mwea! I thought I recognised you!' the woman exclaimed in a clear, musical voice, shaking their hands.

'I could hardly fail to recognise you too, Njambi; you're as lovely as ever.' It was not strictly true. The girl he'd loved had been a smooth black colour; this woman was bleached, and she had a scar on her left cheek. His girl had had neatly combed hair; this one had a wig. His girl had had full curves; this one was thin. Above all his girl's eyes had radiated warmth, but this one's were cold.

'You've grown quite strong yourself,' she said truthfully, since he had been slim then. 'What have you been doing with yourself?'

'Working in the same factory, but it's a big place nowadays. What about you?'

'I've a small business in the city. We're here on a seminar organised by the Mothers' Union of my church.'

'You became religious?' he asked with raised eyebrows.

'Yes, and I find life easier and full.'

He was glad to hear that. 'Why don't you sit down and join us?'

'No, thank you. I'm OK.' She smiled at the girl, who was looking up at her without enthusiasm. 'But won't you introduce your friend?'

'She's our new field supervisor,' Mwea explained simply. He definitely did not want Waithera to know his past women, this one in particular. To his alarm Njambi spoke again.

'I'll be around for a while. I might drop in at the factory for old times' sake. Tell Penina to expect me.'

'I shall,' he muttered uncomfortably.

'I've got to run along now. See you.' She left, waving.

Somehow, Waithera felt the magic of the evening was broken. That strange instinct women have for suspecting past affairs had gripped her. 'It's getting late. I'd like to go home,' she said quietly.

Mwea did not argue. He settled the bill and they left.

Njambi was left walking along the street cursing Waithera. The girl had ruined her plans! Penina, her informant at the factory, had assured her that the man was not going with any woman at the moment. She had been told that he usually stopped at the restaurant, alone, on his way to his home. So Njambi had waited for him there, and would have worked on him, but she had not expected any competition! She had seen him give the girl a certain look; a look that once had been reserved for her only.

What could such a man find so appealing in such a simpleton? Njambi did not want to admit she was envious of the girl's youth and perfection, perfection that did not need any make-up to drive a man wild. She could not admit that, even if the clock was reversed and she was once more of the same age as the girl, Waithera would still outshine her!

But finally she admitted she could not compete with Waithera. There was no way Mwea would be interested in her again as long as he had that stupid girl. But Njambi was not the type to give up at the first obstacle. She began to make new plans to get rid of the competition.

5

Love in Doubt

Waithera spent the following day with her family after the Sunday service. It was relaxing after a busy week, but she was worried about her mother, who looked more frail than usual. She was also worried about her growing relationship with the boss, for she was finding herself liking him against her better judgement, especially after their drive to town the day before. She kept recalling it, and the woman who had approached them.

But on Monday she was too busy for personal matters. She terrorised her leaf-buying clerks in a friendly but firm way, and they in return terrorised the farmers, who soon started grumbling. Their displeasure reached the manager, and he summoned Waithera to his office on Thursday.

She was taken aback to find him looking stern, quite unlike the man she had dated on Saturday. 'Is there anything wrong?' she asked nervously.

'I've been told that you have rejected an average of two tons of leaves daily.'

'That's likely. Why do you ask?'

'Because I've also been told that most of the leaves were OK. I'm waiting for an explanation.'

'What is there to explain, Mr Mwea? If you recall my already approved recommendations, it is part of a strategy. We need to discourage them from bringing the poorest grades. By discouraging I mean rejecting them altogether. Then perhaps they'll sit down and listen when we start educating them.'

'You mean it's deliberate?'

'Yes, and as long as I'm leaf officer we'll keep on rejecting them. The sooner they learn to produce a high grade, the better. I thought you wanted quality?'

'I do,' he agreed, feeling foolish. 'It's just that I didn't understand your uh . . . strategy. Do what you think best. I'll back you, though some of the big boys might throw their weight around.'

'I do sincerely believe it is for the best,' she said, moving to the door. 'Now if you have no further complaints, sir . . .'

'I do have, Miss Wagema. I hardly see you. What about dinner and dance tonight?'

She paused to study him. 'Some other time, Mr Mwea, but you're most welcome to lunch.'

'Accepted,' he said. He could not quite figure her out. She was encouraging and yet discouraging him.

No sooner did he arrive than she invited him to sit down. She brought a bowl of water for him to wash his hands and served up a simple affair of *chapati* with potato and beef stew. She seemed glad to lunch with him.

He took a mouthful. 'Salt and chilli, please,' he asked, then went on. 'Excellent meal,' though he thought she had added too much water to the stew. 'But you know, I'd rather eat you.'

'Cannibalism is prohibited here,' she smiled. 'Be content with food and restrain yourself.'

'OK, lady. But I warn you I can't do so much longer. The urge to maul gets more and more irresistible. When may I get a bite; just a tiny bite?' he asked, touching her lips with a forefinger.

'You're very wicked,' she said softly. 'But you can have your "bite" if you continue being good for a few months.'

'Endure such torture for *months*? How cruel! It is more than flesh and blood can bear.'

'We'll have to bear it, then perhaps we'll know our own minds.'

He noted with excitement that she'd said 'we'. Could it be that she was considering him too? 'I already know what I want,' he protested. 'Something more lasting.'

She ran her fingers lightly and slowly over her smooth features. 'Even after this face is wrinkled? I don't believe you, and that is just the trouble.'

She had cause to doubt him a few minutes later, after he'd left. She was preparing to leave for work when there was a knock on the door.

'Good afternoon,' Waithera said to the tall, slim lady who stood on the doorstep with a boy of about seven. 'I seem to know you. Do you work here?'

'I used to,' said the lady. 'We met at the hotel, remember?'

Waithera had almost forgotten, but now she remembered vividly. It was the woman Mwea had called Njambi, and looked at as if he'd had dealings with her.

'Sorry to bother you,' Njambi went on, 'but I understand you're one of the few with a telephone. May I make a call please?'

'Go ahead, but you'll have to be brief. I'm on my way to work.'

'I won't be a minute.' Njambi tapped out a number while Waithera started talking kindly to the boy. Njambi spoke to her housegirl in Nairobi but her mind was not on the conversation. She was thinking with much pain of the expensive furniture and audio-visual equipment in the room. She had been told Waithera also had a digital oven and fridge, not to mention conveniences like air-conditioning and water heating. Hardly the type of goods a newly employed girl could afford. All of it could have been hers, she thought bitterly.

But she was smiling more brightly than ever as she hung

up the receiver and took the boy's hand. 'Thank you very much.'

'My pleasure,' Waithera replied, picking up her keys and handbag.

Njambi did not move. 'You're nice, you know. I wish you the best of luck.'

'Thanks. But why do you say that?'

'It's just that you appeal to me, for you remind me of myself when I first came here. I wouldn't want you to meet my fate. I met someone whom I thought loved me, for he was very generous to me. Then I conceived his child and he dropped me. I had to leave my job, and I'm still struggling with my child. Still, I find solace in him and religion.'

Njambi was holding the boy as if she wanted Waithera to take a closer look at him. Waithera stared in fascinated horror: he resembled Mwea! That was why the child had looked familiar from the start! Waithera felt sick and faint.

Njambi was pleased with the impact she had made but she pretended to be concerned. 'I'm sorry. I didn't mean to shock you. I meant well, but perhaps it's none of my business.'

'Please go.'

Njambi left, laughing to herself, unaware or perhaps not caring that it was wicked to involve an innocent child in her schemes. Waithera lay down on the sofa to recover her strength and collect her thoughts.

She did not know why she was shocked. She had been warned about Mwea. She had got involved with him knowing him for what he was. But she had not reckoned on coming face to face with his past, the ugly past of a heartless beast who shirked his responsibilities by dropping victims who became pregnant. She was glad she had not committed herself. But why did it hurt so?

'You'll know heaven and hell,' Mama Asha had warned her. But at least she could protect herself from being hurt further by discouraging him totally. Having decided that, she closed the door and left.

Two women watched her through a window. Njambi and her informant, Penina. The latter was a small woman who took up snooping like a hobby. She simply delighted in meddling in other people's affairs, perhaps because nobody wanted her. They watched Waithera walk to the office block, where Mwea was waiting for her. He seemed to talk to her, but she appeared to ignore him, go to her Land Rover and drive away.

The women who were watching looked at each other and laughed. 'It's working as I knew it would!' Njambi exclaimed. 'I knew she was one of those stupid women who expect men to be saints! She is going to be far easier to get rid of than I expected!'

Mwea was puzzled and troubled. He could not understand Waithera's sudden change of attitude towards him. On Thursday she had been friendly enough to invite him to lunch. Now she didn't appear to want to talk to him. She was responsive on business matters, but not on personal ones. She seemed completely indifferent to him as a man.

Penina the snooper noticed this and rang Njambi in town. Njambi was pleased. But she was not going to pounce on her man until she was sure she had effectively eliminated Waithera. She had been careful not to meet him, for she did not want to be blamed. That was why she had not mentioned Mwea's name to Waithera. She could always deny having told the girl she had his child.

She hoped Waithera would not mention the child to Mwea, who did not know about him. When she had been unfaithful to him, she had not realised she was pregnant by him. She only realised after they'd parted, when he'd severed all ties with her. She wanted to tell him about his son herself, after eliminating the girl, then perhaps he would find it easier to forgive her.

It appeared she had succeeded in fixing Waithera, for more days passed without any sign of her softening towards Mwea. He found he could not concentrate on his work. He became moody and lost his appetite. He longed for her smile. Finally he could not bear it any longer. He cast aside his pride and strode purposefully towards her office after a particularly bad night. He found her filling in a ledger surrounded by her team of field clerks.

'Clear off,' he ordered the clerks. 'You can have your figures recorded tomorrow.'

The team left, giving one another knowing looks. Mwea and Waithera were left standing, facing each other. He had not shaved or combed his hair, but she looked neat in a sky blue dress.

'What's wrong, Mr Mwea?' she asked nervously, seeing the look on his face.

'Don't "mister" me!'

'All right, but I assure you the farmers are learning fast, and we're now rejecting less than a ton.'

'I want to know what I have done to deserve this.'

'Deserve what?'

'You know damn well that you've been ignoring me.'

Seeing how serious and troubled he was, she did not deny it. She wondered if he was really rough and haggard because of her. She looked him straight in the face and said, 'I don't want to talk about it, please. However, I must tell you I was hoping we could go on being friends, and develop mutual trust and something else, but now I find that is impossible. It is best we have nothing to do with each other outside work. Please don't make it difficult for me. I like it here and I don't want to have to leave.'

He was dismayed. Whatever had come between them must

be serious. Sickly frustration filled him. 'Has someone been poisoning your mind against me? I know I have a bad reputation, but that is all in the past. I even confessed it to you when we were fishing.'

'You didn't confess everything!' she retorted. 'What is more, I don't take heed of gossip, but I do believe my own eyes!'

'What can you have seen?' he asked, more bewildered than ever. 'I don't remember even noticing another woman since I first saw you.'

'I said I don't want to talk about it. What I saw, I saw. Now may I go on with my work please?'

Remembering he had been warned she could be stubborn, he decided to leave her alone for the present.

Njao, Waithera's brother, came to see her with bad tidings three days later, to add more distress to her already troubled mind. He came before she went to work and broke the news after breakfast.

'Mother's health has worsened, Waithera,' he informed her. 'We took her to the dispensary yesterday, but they could only recommend special treatment in a private hospital. You know the old man is broke. He cannot raise the kind of money required. He tried to borrow from friends last night, but he had no luck. He doesn't want to bother you since you gave him half your first salary last week, but I thought I'd come and tell you in case there is anything you can do.'

'You say she has to be hospitalised?' Waithera asked in dismay.

'I am afraid so.'

'Good God!' She sank into a chair.

'It's terrible, isn't it?' Njao continued. 'Just when my admission letter has arrived from college. I am expected in two weeks, failing which my place will be taken by another.

But of course I'll have to forget it now since Mother must be taken care of first.'

This increased Waithera's gloom. But her mind was busy. If only Mama Asha was around, she would have helped her a bit. The only other person who could help her was Mwea, but she did not want to involve him in personal matters, and she had told him as much. But first things first. Her mother had to be treated. She would worry about the bills later.

She went to the 'phone and tapped out a number, hoping the person she was calling had arrived early as usual. He had. 'Hello. Waithera here. I wish to request a day off. Mother is ill.'

'Not seriously I hope?' said the low, manly voice at the other end.

'It is serious, sir, for she has to be hospitalised. I also wish to request use of the Land Rover to take her.'

There was a pause at the other end. 'Come over when you're ready,' the voice said, and hung up.

Waithera did not know what to make of it, but she was sure that her request would not be denied. What she had not expected was to find him waiting with his Pajero, ready to take her personally.

'This is awfully kind of you, Mwea,' she told him, genuinely grateful, whatever his motive. 'But we shouldn't put you to so much trouble.'

'No trouble at all. We have to share sorrow as well as joy. I want you to believe that, Waithera.'

She was about to reply when she glanced at her brother who quickly thanked Mwea for them both. 'Now if you'll let me see my assistant . . .'

'I've already told him to take over,' he told her, 'just as I have instructed my own.'

The three of them drove to Waithera's farm. The old people were awed to see their daughter brought in a heavy car by the big man himself. They wondered, and they hoped, since she had never brought a man home. When they learned of the purpose of his visit, they heaped him with blessings in a way which made him uncomfortable. They were far more grateful than their suspicious daughter.

'This calls for more than a bottle, young man,' her father said. 'You must let me slaughter a goat for you one of these days.'

'And I shall make him my best in powdered food,' Waithera's mother put in feebly as she sat on her stool, leaning against the wall.

'But first you will have to get well, Mammi,' said Waithera. 'Come and help me get her to the car, Njao.'

As their mother was helped into the back seat, Mwea looked at her. She was so thin and weak. Then he looked at the incomplete house and sympathised with the old man. Waithera stayed in the back seat to support her mother while Njao sat on the passenger seat beside the driver. The old man was left to take care of the home. Mwea started the vehicle, engaged four-wheel drive and it roared up the steep drive to the main road above.

It was a tedious journey to the hospital, which was in another district, especially for the invalid. It was a neat missionary hospital in beautiful grounds on the outskirts of a small town. The old lady was examined and admitted. She was to undergo intensive tests with a special diet for her diabetes. Waithera filled in and signed some forms, knowing the treatment was going to be expensive.

'Truly, to give birth is a blessing,' the old lady whispered, smiling weakly as she was half carried away by a couple of nurses.

'Goodbye, Mammi,' said Waithera, holding back tears. 'I'll come to see you often.'

Mwea took brother and sister for a late lunch at the nearby town. They were pretty quiet; Mwea tried to distract them by talking of commonplace matters.

Waithera was grateful for her brother's presence, though her own problem with Mwea had receded to the back of her mind. She was too engrossed with her mother's sickness, which had been part of her life since she was young. She wondered how much longer the old lady would survive. Then there was the problem of the hospital bill and her brother's education. But later, after they had driven back and had dropped Njao off at the farm, she found herself alone with Mwea. He saw her need to think, and he did not bother her with talk. It was evening as they drove back to the factory. He escorted her to the front of her house.

'There's no need to be so glum, Waithera,' he told her kindly. 'She's in good hands. Everything will be all right.'

'Do you really think so, Mwea?'

He could see her pleading face looking up at him in the lights. 'Yes, my dear, I do.'

She leaned against him, her cheek on his shoulder. It was merely the impulsive gesture of someone seeking reassurance, but the feel of her lovely, feminine body against his set him on fire. His mind whirled like one dazed. His strong arms closed around her gently, and she did not resist, for the embrace gave her a feeling of being protected which she needed badly. He hugged her and felt a sweet tremor shake him to the core of his being, as it had when he had held her before. His lips found her smooth cheek, kissed it and proceeded to her slightly parted lips. She sighed; her body pressed against his manly one. Mwea felt as if the world had melted away and he was in a heaven of excitement.

'This, then, is true love,' he heard himself mutter.

His words shook her back to reality. The flame he had lit in her went out. She placed her hands on his chest. 'No, it isn't true,' she said, and pushed him away. 'You've had your bite. Now leave me alone. I have enough problems without having my life ruined as well.'

He knew he had taken advantage of her moment of

weakness, and he reluctantly let go of her. 'You really believe I can ruin you?'

'Yes, with reason. Now please go, but thanks for everything else.'

'OK, I'll go,' he said in frustration, 'but if you think the matter ends there, Emma Waithera, you're mistaken.'

As he left, other eyes apart from Waithera's watched him. Penina the snooper was in the shadows a few blocks away. She entered her house, put on a coat and went to a telephone booth at a shopping centre which was a kilometre or two away. She could hardly wait to tell the news; the type which delighted her meddling nature.

'They are together again!' she said after the call was through. 'They spent all day together. I actually saw them kissing each other! I believe they'll spend the night together also,' she added mischievously.

'Whaat . . . ?' Njambi exclaimed in fury. She went on to call Waithera the names of some animals, none of which was nice. 'I must have miscalculated somewhere,' she went on and her voice was without its musical quality. 'I forgot to take the man into consideration. He is aggressive and could have easily wooed the stupid mongoose of a girl back! He must be discouraged! I'll have to think carefully before I strike again, and this time I won't make any mistakes!'

6

Nightmare Date

Waithera became more worried and tense as the days passed. Worried because her mother did not improve. Tense because with each passing day the hospital bill got higher. Her frequent trips to the hospital used the little money she had. Then there was her brother. The deadline to raise his admission fees was getting closer.

She tried to forget all this by working harder. She had undertaken the first step of the gigantic task of improving quality by rejecting tons of leaves. The next step was going to be just as unpopular, for there was going to be more pruning and tending the soil than leaf picking. She went to the chief, who organised a series of meetings presided over by the local Agricultural Officer.

Mwea attended two of the meetings and was impressed by the way she was persuading the farmers. The campaign was quite effective. Demand for fertiliser increased four-fold; there was mass pruning and cultivation. Unfortunately, the pruning made production drop by by thirty per cent. This worried Mwea, and he went to see Waithera.

'The loss is staggering. This project of yours is more expensive than I expected. Remember, this is the low season, and we're operating below capacity as it is.'

'I'm sorry, but it can't be helped,' Waithera replied. 'When the long rains come, we'll not only have better quality, but the greatest quantity ever.'

'I hope so, or you and I might be out of jobs.'

'It won't fail unless the rains do.' She smiled gratefully at him. 'Thank you for your support.'

He was glad she could still smile. To the world she presented her usual cheerful face, but he could sense the sadness and tension beneath. He felt for her, and wished she would confide in him, but she wouldn't. There was still a barrier between them, even if she had been more friendly towards him ever since he had taken her mother to the hospital. He also wished he could take her in his arms again, but he could not do that, for he had come to feel guilty for having taken advantage by kissing her in such a manner when she was so unhappy. When he did so again, he wanted her to be happy and willing, but he feared such a time was far off.

Njambi was worried as she walked to the public telephone booth. Her own phone had been disconnected two days earlier. She knew the electricity was the next to go. At least she had paid for the water, but of what use would it be to her if she was evicted, as she would be if she defaulted for yet another month? She had to stop dragging her feet and secure Mwea for herself. But before she could get him she had to discourage him from desiring Waithera.

Knowing him as Njambi did, the only sure way of making him detest his woman was to find her with another man. She had cause to know this since he had cut her from his life for that reason. Waithera had to have a few men somewhere, and Mwea had to catch her with one of them. Penina knew about everybody's sex life in the factory, and it was she Njambi was going to call as they had arranged.

'Hello, Penina!' she said when she had her friend on the line. 'How are things there?'

'They are still together, but not much.'

'What do you mean?'

'I mean they don't appear close. They don't go out together or that sort of thing. I hear the woman has a patient in a hospital and doesn't seem to have much time for the man.'

Njambi was relieved to hear that. 'What about him? Is he still keen on her?'

'Very. He always stops her to talk to her.'

'Then he must be discouraged as I said. Now tell me, Penina, and it's important – how many boyfriends does she have in or out of the factory?'

'I know of only one: the boss.'

Njambi was disappointed to hear that. 'You mean with her looks no one is interested in her?'

'Most of the men are wild about her. You should hear them talk. But they dare not displease the boss.'

'Are you absolutely sure nobody else visits her house?'

'Not anybody I know of.'

'Then make friends with her. Introduce her to another man from outside. You're a woman. He doesn't have to be rich and handsome. An experienced, sweet-talking wencher will do.'

'Mboche, the factory's womaniser, tried her, and she just laughed him off. I tell you the little interest she has for men is for Mwea.'

'And I tell you she has to be fixed somehow,' Njambi insisted. 'It looks as if I'll have to come over there and do it myself.'

♥

Ten days after taking her mother to the hospital, Waithera was utterly relieved to find she was resting under the shade outside with others. She was out of danger, the doctor assured her, and was making steady recovery.

That removed the worst burden from Waithera's mind. But it meant the time to settle the bill was approaching fast. It made her more desperate than ever, and she had not yet thought of a solution. Finally she decided she had no choice but to swallow her pride, go to Mwea, and borrow from him, no matter how long it took to repay him. She didn't know if he had that kind of ready money on him, but somehow she knew he would find a way. She also knew he was genuine enough to want to help her. Her decision made her find sleep at last.

But as she went to see him in his office in the morning, she stopped to think. It was not fair to take advantage of his desire for her. Not unless they were betrothed, and they never would be. Not after the way he had treated Njambi and others. She could give in for the sake of convenience, but she just wasn't made that way. She couldn't do it even for her mother. So she returned to her house, more worried than ever.

But in the afternoon she received a letter which cheered her a bit. Now at least she could get advice and comfort. She made a long distance call in the morning, and it was some time before someone came on the line.

'Hello,' said a small voice.

'Asha!' Waithera cried in delight. 'How are you, dear?'

'Auntie Waithera! Auntie Waithera!' shrieked the little one in joy. 'Where are you?'

'At the factory, Asha. Where is Mummy, Asha?'

'Outside.'

'Go and call her. Put the telephone you're holding on the table. Don't put it where it was.'

The mother's gentle voice came on the line presently. 'Is it really you, Waithera? How I've missed you!'

'Not as much as I've missed you. I got your letter yesterday and called the first moment I could.'

'I'm glad. Tell me, what has been happening since I left? What's been happening between you and Mwea?'

'He's been nice to me,' Waithera replied, not knowing exactly how to express herself, 'and decent – almost,' she added, remembering how he'd lost control and grabbed her twice. 'He still seems to want me, but I don't trust him.'

Mama Asha was sad to hear that, since Mwea had assured

her that he was sincere. Waithera did not tell her friend how she'd met one of his victims. She went on to talk about her mother's illness and her brother's fees, and asked for advice. Mama Asha sympathised and considered for a while. Then she said, 'Within a few years I'll be able to help you on such matters with ease, Waithera, but right now all we had has gone into developing this property. In fact, we're heavily in debt ourselves. However, I'll think over what can be done and call you back.'

Mwea's phone trilled softly and musically ten minutes later. He was pleased to hear Mama Asha on the line, but not so pleased when she said, 'You know, I'm disappointed in you, Mwea. You assured me you were sincere with Waithera. Did you know that her mother was recovering in a hospital?'

'I ought to know. I helped Waithera to take her there.'

'Fine. But are you aware that the treatment is expensive?'

'It did cross my mind, but she hasn't asked for my help.'

'She wouldn't, but if you cared enough, you wouldn't let her suffer to the extent of calling all the way to me for advice.'

He was silent for a moment. 'I see; she wouldn't confide in me. I'm nothing to her,' he declared bitterly. 'So don't blame me. If she doesn't need my help, why should I bother?'

'Of course she needs your help, but she isn't the type to go moaning about her problems to just anyone, only to those who are close to her. There must be something preventing her from getting close to you. She called you almost decent. But she is suspicious of you – she didn't say why – but it's up to you to search your conscience.'

'She puzzles me, you know. Sometimes she is friendly, but most of the time she's distant. If only she'd talk!'

'She will, in her own time. In the meantime, are you going to act, or do I have to come over there and organise a fund-raising drive myself?'

Waithera spent most of her free time near the phone. Mama Asha had not promised her anything concrete, but in her desperation she had no other hope to cling to. She trusted her friend enough to believe she would think of something. But the day passed, and the next without a word from Mama Asha. But on the third day, just when Waithera was about to despair, the phone rang. She grabbed it, and was relieved to hear it was Mama Asha.

'I should have known you wouldn't forsake me!'

'Everything has been arranged. Now listen carefully. Go to your father immediately. Take him to the tea growers' co-operative society, of which he is a member. You're to fill in forms applying for a loan not exceeding six thousand pounds, repayable in three years. Don't look for a guarantor. Just leave the forms there. A friend of mine will guarantee them later. The old man can collect the cheque after a week. It ought to be enough to pay the hospital bill, take your brother to college and finish building the house, don't you think?'

Waithera was speechless. 'I – I must be dreaming!' she gasped finally. 'It's too marvellous to be true!'

'Of course it's true. I wouldn't lie to you, would I?'

As the realisation sunk in, Waithera's face lit up and she gave a cry of sheer joy.

'*Ee-yu-hu*! May God bless you and your family, and give you long, long life to go on doing good to the world.'

Mama Asha felt a little uncomfortable, for it was really Mwea who was to be thanked. It was he who was going to see the loan through with his influence and personal guarantee.

'I hope there will be no problem with repayment?'

'I don't think so. Father and I can manage it in three years.'

Ten minutes later, Waithera burst into Mwea's office, smiling brightly, looking lively and enthusiastic. He looked up from the morning paper and watched her as she came right up to his desk. Her eyes were sparkling, her bright face was radiant. It was as if she had brought sunlight and cheer to his office. Her left hand snatched away his paper and her right one shook his warmly. 'Good morning, Mwea! You arrive so early. Do you ever take breakfast?'

'Good morning, Waithera. I'm glad to see you looking happy for a change.'

'Yes, I'm happy. Mother is better and we'll be able to pay. Permission to go home, please, sir?'

'It depends for what, Waithera.'

'Mama Asha has arranged for Father to get a loan. I am to take him to the co-operative office to apply. Marvellous, isn't it?'

'Almost as marvellous as yourself when you're happy, my dear.'

'Not as much as yourself if you'll let me go.'

'I never, never will, Emma Waithera. But I suppose I can let you see your father until noon.'

She patted his cheek and gave him back his paper. 'You're sweet. Have a nice day.' She left.

He was left touching where her hand had patted his cheek, smiling to himself. It was really worthwhile to see her happy. It was sufficient reward for the effort he had made on her behalf. But he wondered if she would be so eager if she knew it was he and not Mama Asha who had made the deal.

♥

Things ran smoothly for Waithera for once. At work there was definite improvement of quality. All that was needed now was rain to increase production. At the hospital her mother regained her strength steadily. At home her brother prepared for college, while at the society the loan went through without a hitch.

Her only problem was Mwea. He seemed to mistake her cheerful mood as a sign that she was softening towards him. He tried to date her and she politely declined, for now there was no question of their getting acquainted enough to develop something more lasting. Njambi had proved him to be untrustworthy. It was such a pity, though, since she had come to admire and like his other qualities.

As for Mwea, the more she frustrated him, the more he yearned for her. Never before had he spent so much time and energy in the pursuit of a woman. Waithera had become an obsession with him. Perhaps she really had bewitched him. Now that her mother was not on her mind so much, he would renew his assault on her. The first step was to find out why she had suddenly withdrawn from him after the time she had invited him to lunch. She had declined to talk about it, but this time he would insist. He called her on the phone.

'Look here, Waithera,' he began. 'It's important we talk. I won't take no for an answer this time. Can I pick you up after work? We could go to a small, quiet little town I know where we can chat.'

There was silence at the other end. 'Hello! Waithera! Did you hear me?'

'I heard you, Mwea,' her smooth voice replied. 'I'll come on condition that it will be just as a friend.'

'OK. Just say you'll be ready by six.'

'All right,' she murmured, and hung up.

He did the same, but the phone trilled moments later. He picked up the receiver again, and a hoarse voice said, 'Hello! The manager?'

'Speaking. Who is calling please?'

'I am on leave from headquarters. First let me congratulate you on the success you've made of the factory. But I've spotted a slight mistake: misuse of corporation vehicles. Some of your staff go to drink with them. I have, for instance, noticed a certain Land Rover, KYX 244, outside a bar twice.'

Mwea stiffened. It was Waithera's vehicle. 'You're mistaken. The officer in charge of that one doesn't drink.'

The voice laughed. 'I'm positive. Check it at Muturi bar

this evening. I heard them arranging them to meet there again.'

'Look here, whoever you are,' Mwea said in irritation, 'I appreciate your concern, but you're wrong. Good day.'

He hung up, wondering who the caller was – obviously crazy for suggesting Waithera drank. Unlike the other officers who had the privilege of a vehicle, she never, never went anywhere outside work without his permission. Perhaps it was her driver who went drinking with the Land Rover. It was unlikely, but he would check it out, since he could not risk having an alcoholic for her driver.

Mwea spent the rest of the day moving around the factory, inspecting the various sections, and planning how to persuade Waithera to speak her mind.

Meanwhile, Waithera was thinking about him. She was at a remote collection centre, coaching a new boy. She felt instinctively what Mwea wanted them to discuss, but she did not relish talking about or even remembering his past, which had ruined their relationship.

A young man came up to her on a bicycle. He was wearing a green dustcoat like most of the factory workers. 'Excuse me, Miss Wagema. Mr Mwea sent me to tell you to meet him at five this evening at the Muturi bar and restaurant.'

'Where on earth is it?'

'It's that two-storey building over there,' he said, pointing at a small shopping centre on top of one of the hills.

'Why didn't he contact me by the radio instead of sending you all the way?'

'I met him on the road. He said you are to wait for him there, where he is meeting a friend. You're to go straight there without returning to the factory.'

'I see.' But she could not quite see why he had suddenly changed the time and venue for their date, without even giving her time to go home to take a shower and change.

However, at four-thirty she told the driver to take her to

the Muturi restaurant. It was a tiny, one-street town. The only modern building was the two-storey hotel-bar. Leaving the driver in the Land Rover, she entered the building and grimaced in distaste. It was more of a bar than a restaurant, and very noisy. It was tolerably clean, but the yelling patrons did not impress her, especially after she was instantly offered a drink and money for certain favours. She was about to walk out again when a stout, balding well-dressed man approached her.

'Emma Waithera I presume? Come this way please,' he told her in a hoarse but polite voice. 'Mwea called to tell me to expect you.'

'Where is he?'

'On the way. He got held up by work at the factory.'

'Who are you?'

'George. I do business with him.'

'I'll wait for him outside in the vehicle.'

George smiled in understanding. 'It's all right. Mwea has ordered a private table for you.'

She reluctantly let him lead her to a room at the rear, where there was just a table and some chairs. But at least there was privacy, though she could still hear the yelling at the front. They sat down.

'What kind of business do you do with him, if I may ask?'

'Oh, he wants to grab some shares from me, just as he grabbed a plot. But this time I won't let him get them so cheaply.'

A barmaid appeared, and the man ordered two beers, explaining that Mwea had said the drinks would be on him. 'Just a Fanta for me,' said Waithera, regretting having gone there. There was something not quite right.

However, the man was polite as they sipped and waited. Waithera kept listening for Mwea's Pajero, though there were no vehicles to be heard. Finally they heard one.

'Check if that's his car,' the man said.

'It doesn't sound like it.' Waithera went to the window to check all the same. She did not notice him slip something into her drink, and he joined her at the window to distract her even more as it dissolved.

'It's just a pick-up with potato vanes,' she said.

'I hope he doesn't keep us waiting much longer.'

'So do I,' she said, 'because I'm leaving as soon as I finish my soda.'

She sat down again and went on sipping, and if she thought it tasted a bit odd, she did not suspect anything or make a comment. But after she had drained her glass and tried to rise, she felt her limbs getting heavy, and her mind drowsy. She held her head.

'Are you OK, Waithera?'

'I – I feel strange. I've got to go. I have to.'

Collecting her fading strength, she staggered to her feet and he rose also. She took two steps, stopped, swayed like one dazed and then tumbled. George caught her before she fell on the floor and lowered her back on to her chair, where she lay motionless. He filled her glass with beer and proceeded to force a little of it into her mouth and down her throat.

Meanwhile, Mwea was waiting for her at the factory. He kept pacing around the front of the office block, looking up the drive now and then. But there was no sign of the Land Rover. He also kept looking at his watch and saw how late she was. Maybe there was too much work or the vehicle had broken down. But he soon admitted he was making excuses for her. She simply had no intention of turning up for their date, and was staying away until he got tired of waiting and left. This made him annoyed, for she should have declined as she had done before, and he would have accepted it.

Or maybe the driver had caused the delay by drinking, as Mwea had been warned. This was highly unlikely, since it was she and not the driver who was in charge, but he decided to check. He went to his car, started it and made for Muturi bar. He had drunk there once and he had not liked it.

He drove up and down a few hills to the place and had a shock: the Land Rover *was* there, parked in front of the bar. Seated behind the wheel was the driver, looking bored but otherwise quite sober. The uniformed, elderly man became alert as the white Pajero pulled up beside him.

'What on earth are you doing here?' Mwea snapped.

'Waiting, as you can see, sir.'

'Where is she?'

'In there,' the driver replied uncomfortably, since he believed like everybody else Waithera was Mwea's.

Mwea looked at the bar in disbelief. 'Are you sure? Are you in the habit of taking her to bars?'

'Never, Mr Mwea. But today she ordered me to bring her here, and I did.'

'Did she say why?'

'To see you.'

'To see me?' Mwea gasped. He could not believe all this. It was just a mistake – or a nightmare. His angel could not tell such a lie. She couldn't break their date to go to a beer hall. She could not repeat what Njambi had done to him once. He did not want to think of the warning he had received that morning; that she had arranged to have a drink here with someone else. He got out of the Pajero, slammed the door and left it in the middle of the road.

He stamped into the bar. His bristling look made even the noisy customers fall silent. He glanced round the bar through narrowed eyes, but he did not see Waithera. Maybe she was in the lodging rooms upstairs. He went to the barmaid behind the counter.

'I want the woman with the Land Rover.'

'Sorry. That one is engaged. Try another.'

'I said I want to see her!' Mwea hissed. 'Where is she?'

The woman trembled. 'In the back room.'

'With whom?'

'A fellow who was waiting for her.'

Mwea strode to the rear room, flung the door open and stood surveying the scene before him, which was unimaginable even in a nightmare. His 'angel' was seated and asleep, supported by a stout, half bald fellow who had a glass of beer in one hand while the other was round her, fondling her breasts.

No words could describe Mwea's feelings. Suffice to say his utter shock, bitterness and fury made his vision blurred, then he saw red. Slowly his sight returned, but his wrath remained.

'Don't open the door,' Waithera's sugar-daddy told him. 'She just passed out after the fourth bottle, you know. Probably not used to drinking much. I don't like them drunk, do you? They don't respond; they just lie like logs.'

The man realised he had overdone his part, for his dirty hand and words made Mwea strip off his jacket and fold back his shirtsleeves, looking as friendly and harmless as a hangman. 'Will you die outside, mister,' he breathed, 'or right here? Take a choice, quickly! I don't have all evening.'

'Look here!' the man said, rising to his feet in panic, leaving Waithera lying across the two chairs, 'I didn't know she was yours! I was only trying my luck as anyone would.'

Seeing Mwea was not listening, he whipped out a knife and charged with a snarl. He was a powerful man, but no match for the more finely built Mwea, who swiftly grabbed his wrist with his left hand, rendering the knife harmless, and swung his right fist back, to drive it on to the fellow's jaw with the force of a sledgehammer. The heavy man went sprawling over the table, breaking it and shattering the bottles and glasses on it, then crashed head first against the wall opposite before he fell on the floor with an impact which shook the room. He lay there, quite still.

The commotion brought people rushing into the room. Mwea ignored them and put on his jacket. Then he bent over the girl, who smelt of beer and appeared to be in a drunken stupor. He turned away from her in disgust, and was about to walk out of the room when a barmaid blocked his way, yelling about the damage. He gave her some notes, brushed her aside and walked outside.

'Go home,' he told the driver, who started the Land Rover and drove off. Mwea got into his car and started it also. He engaged gear, thought better of it and stopped the vehicle. He thought for a while and then got out of it.

He entered the bar again, to return carrying the unconscious girl in his arms. People watched as he dumped her on the rear seat. Then he returned to his seat and drove off.

Njambi and Penina watched him go from behind a wall. Then they hurried to the back room of the bar, where Njambi was dismayed to find the mess and the unconscious man. She had him carried to a room upstairs, where she bandaged his smashed jaw and nursed him back to consciousness. He was a gangster from the city whom she had always rejected until now, when she needed his services.

'You didn't warn me he was violent,' he complained angrily, his hoarse voice weak.

'He never was!' she protested. 'Tell me what actually happened.'

Slowly, painfully, he told her what had occurred from the time he had met Waithera to when Mwea had stormed in.

'I didn't tell you to touch her or to talk that way to him!' Njambi scolded him. 'How else did you expect him to react, you stupid gorilla? I just wanted you to give the impression that she had been drinking with you.'

'I was only trying to be realistic.'

'Too realistic,' she told him scornfully. 'But perhaps it's good for me even if it was bad for you, for he's not likely to desire her after this. I'll have to wait for his reaction.'

7

Angel in Disgrace

Waithera gradually became conscious of something hard and cold pressing against her. The cold! Her whole body was cold. Her eyes opened slightly, but her mind was numb. She became aware of a dark figure with a hat and an overcoat towering over her. Then a bright beam of light fell on her eyes, blinding her. She tried to scream but made no sound.

'She is waking up!' a voice said as if from the distance. 'Don't be frightened Waithera. Wake up; you've got to wake up!'

Waithera stirred and looked around her, but she could not sit up. She was lying on her verandah and it was night. A watchman was bent over her while several other people looked on. 'You can't sleep outside. You'll die of cold. You must get inside. Where are your keys?'

She tried to grasp the message. 'Purse,' she whispered. The night-watchman could not see one, but after a search he felt it down her back under her dress, where someone must have shoved it. He called one of the women who was watching to retrieve it and open the door. Then he called another of the women to help the first one get Waithera inside. The girl felt herself being carried, undressed and tucked up in her comfortable bed. Then she knew nothing more as she slipped back into a deep sleep.

♥

Meanwhile, in an hotel room in Nyeri provincial town, Mwea was also being helped to bed, by a waiter. He was drunk to the point of blackout, just as he had wanted, to drown his bitterness and sorrow. After dumping Waithera on her verandah, he had decided he couldn't go home and face a sleepless night. So he'd gone to the hotel he'd once taken her to and drunk himself silly.

When he woke up in the morning, the pain in his heart was as acute as ever. The vision of Waithera in the arms of the balding fellow was as vivid as ever. The whisky had only succeeded in postponing his agony, and given him a hangover into the bargain. He took some pills and a shower and dressed himself. He ordered tea with fried eggs, felt a little better and found himself able to think about things more clearly. Uppermost in his mind was the fact that he was through with love.

Love! It was no use denying the fact that he was hopelessly in love with Waithera. How else could he explain his violent reaction last night? What of his extreme yearning and concern for her? His day had never been complete without a glimpse of her. She had affected him fully from the start, when she had dropped into his office, looking at him in wide-eyed innocence. He recalled her now, smiling cheerfully or sadly . . . and electrifying his entire being with a simple touch.

But he had been wrong about her. She had almost convinced him of her innocence. Now she had proved to be even worse than Njambi. What on earth had the sugar-daddy been able to offer her that he couldn't? Was she the type that preferred elderly men? Or had she been acting hard to get with him? She made him sick!

Well, he was not going to waste any more of his time on stupid love for females. He would remain a bachelor. Eventually he might take just any woman to bear him a child or two, or he might just simply adopt a child. In the meantime, women would be simply his playthings. Any except Waithera, who would have no role in his life at all. He would fire her.

But later, as he was drafting the dismissal letter in his office, he found he was letting personal matters influence his decision. She would have to be dealt with as any other member of staff would be.

Meanwhile, Waithera was at last waking up. She was dismayed to find it was already half past ten in the morning. She was puzzled by this, since she had never been so late for work. She had a vague memory of herself lying on the verandah and being carried to bed – probably in a dream. Then she remembered going to meet Mwea in a bar and meeting someone else instead. She could remember nothing more, and this made her more puzzled.

She got out of bed. Her mind was foggy, but otherwise she felt all right. She felt even better after a shower and breakfast. It was as she was dressing that she recalled everything clearly. Mwea's friend had ordered a soda for her, and she had passed out. Drugged! But why? Had she been robbed? No, her watch and purse were there. Had her body been violated? She felt OK. But what had happened after she had passed out? And how had she got here? She was going to find out!

As she made for the offices she noticed that people were staring at her as if she had sprouted horns or something. She did not know that the story was all over the factory. The boss had caught her drinking with another man and had gone beserk. The scandal delighted the women, Penina especially, for they were envious of the favours Waithera had been given.

The clerks in the outer office fell silent as she entered, and now she was sure that people had been talking about her. It made her uneasy and she began to wonder again exactly what had happened the night before. She ignored them all and made for the inner office, where the short, thickset personnel manager called to her. She went to his desk.

'You wish to talk to me Mr Mbuchi?'

'Not exactly,' he replied. Waithera realised he was not in his usual jovial mood. He produced a letter from his desk and gave it to her. 'I just wanted to give you this.'

Uneasily Waithera opened the letter at once. It was a warning. It alleged she had been found drinking after work while she was in charge of a factory vehicle. Her driver had confirmed she had directed him to take her to the bar. She was to refrain from such gross misuse of KTDA (Kenya Tea Development Authority) property, failing which she would be dismissed without further warning. The letter was signed by the personnel manager.

She stared at the letter in disbelief, then anger. 'This isn't fair! I went there with reason. I only took a soda, anyhow, and I know the rest of you go on drinking orgies often. Why pick on me?'

'You can always deny it,' he said. 'But I warn you we have proof.'

She went away from him in disgust and burst into Mwea's office. She was taken aback to find he was not his usual polite self, but cold towards her, and his eyes were bloodshot. But since she was not feeling polite herself, she went to his desk and slammed the letter down in front of him. 'I want to know the meaning of this,' she snapped.

He barely glanced at it, as if he knew its contents. 'You want it simplified?' he sneered.

She erupted angrily. 'How dare you let them insult me! You send me to a bar, where your friend is waiting for me with a drugged soda, and then you have me warned! It is too much.'

Mwea looked puzzled. 'What are you talking about?'

She stamped on the floor with her foot, more furious than ever. 'I'm talking about the cyclist you sent to tell me to go to the bar! I'm talking about the beast who drugged me into a coma! Traitor! If you were fed up with me, why didn't you just tell me to quit?'

'Have you gone quite crazy, Waithera? Do you think you can get away with such bubbling, wild explanations? Do you deny having taken one beer too many last night?'

She stamped on the floor again. 'Of course I deny it! I've taken only two glasses of alcohol in my life. The first time was when I stole a glass of beer from Father out of curiosity, long ago. It tasted bitter and I didn't like it. The second time was when you yourself gave me a glass of wine recently. I took it only because you thought it OK for me to do so.'

He shot to his feet, and he was as furious as she. 'Don't act innocent with me any longer; it won't work! Can't you see? I caught you red-handed, dead drunk in the arms of your sugar-daddy! You seem unaware that I personally took you home.'

'You did?'

'Yes. Sorry I took you away from your lover, not that he would have been of much use to you after what I did to him.'

'And you left me on the verandah when I was sick?' Waithera continued more quietly though she was feeling even more bitter. 'And you believed I was drunk, and worse, with someone else?' She started weeping. 'What do you take me for?'

'For what you are,' he replied, also quietly. 'I take back whatever I may have told you in my ignorance. You may be the incarnation of beauty, but it is now marred before my eyes, for your behaviour is not that of my paragon of womanhood. You can't imagine how disappointed I am in you, Emma Waithera.'

He sat down again and picked up the letter. 'As for this, you should consider yourself lucky that you've got off with just a warning. Of course you're free to drink anything, anywhere, with anyone you please outside working hours, but not when you're in charge of a KTDA vehicle. When I took you out in the Pajero, it was because it is my personal property.'

She was too hurt by his unjust accusations to protest any more. She just went on weeping and left.

Penina the snooper enjoyed herself thoroughly for the next few days since Waithera continued to be the talk of the place. Apart from meddling, nothing delighted Penina more than such a scandal. Though she had no grudge against the girl, it was interesting to watch her sudden fall from grace.

Mwea became indifferent, even contemptuous of her. He no longer stopped her whenever he saw her. No longer did he seek her out in the field, or wait to see her after work. He left early, as he had done before she came. When he did talk to her, it was in the same curt way as to anybody else. Perhaps he was even more sharp with her.

As for Waithera, she looked totally humbled. She no longer went to the manager's office as if it was her own. She went about her work with less confidence. She became withdrawn and rarely talked with anyone. After work she just shut herself up in her house.

Her team of field clerks began to slacken, since they no longer feared her. Her fellow senior officers ceased to handle her with care. Even the hungry foxes of the factory, who had kept their distance, considered closing in on her. Mboche, the factory Casanova, especially, started planning to buy her a beer as well, since she was a pushover after all.

Penina the snooper prepared to contact Njambi, to tell her that her plan had worked well beyond expectations. Emma Waithera was definitely no longer special.

Mwea refilled his glass of whisky and sipped it slowly. He had already drunk half the bottle. He was in his regular evening hotel, where he had become an habitual drinker – the type people call DDO (daily drinking officer). He had also become a human chimney, finishing a full packet of cigarettes in one day when before he had only smoked two or three. He had known Waithera only for a short while, but now he realised it would take him a long, long time to get her out of his system.

He was brooding over what might have been when he heard someone call him. He looked up to see a tall, slim woman with a small boy smiling down at him. Her dark face held bitter-sweet memories for him. Sometime back he would not have wanted to see her, but now it didn't matter. Somehow, her crime against him had paled beside Waithera's.

'Hello, Njambi. Don't tell me you're still in town.'

'I only returned yesterday,' she lied, 'to visit a sister in Christ I met during the seminar. I thought I'd come here, hoping to be lucky enough to see you, so I'm glad I came.'

Mwea raised his eyebrows. 'You wished to see me?'

'Yes, Mwea. I've been anxious to know how you were getting along. We didn't get a chance to talk last time.'

Mwea didn't mind talking with her, in fact, he was rather curious about her, too. He invited her to sit on the chair opposite. He looked at the boy, who was staring at him. He stared back. 'Your son I presume?'

'My only one,' she replied, smiling at the boy fondly. 'Say "hi" to the man and go and sit over there.'

'You got married?' Mwea asked after he had ordered snacks for both mother and son.

'I'll tell you. But first tell me about yourself.'

'I've got along,' Mwea explained simply. 'After you jilted me I fell apart, but I managed to pull myself together and buried myself in work.' He was amazed he could talk so casually about it now. 'What about you?'

Njambi looked sad. 'I don't know which devil got into me to do what I did, Mwea, but I soon regretted it. I tried to contact you to tell you how sorry I was, but you wouldn't see me. So I devoted my life to my church, where I could repent and shape myself into a more worthwhile person. I've also waited for a chance to apologise for having wronged you, and this is as good as any.'

Mwea felt uncomfortable. 'All that's in the past, Njambi. I forgive you if it will make you feel better, though I won't forget. Tell me what you're doing nowadays instead.'

'When I'm not on church matters I run a general kiosk. However, high inflation has reduced the stock. I'm finding it difficult to bring up our son.'

'Yours with who?' he asked sharply.

She looked at him, then at the boy. 'Are you blind?'

Mwea *had* detected some resemblance to himself, but thought it coincidental. But the fact that the boy must have been born around the time he had been with his mother made it likely. For the first time he was moved. 'Good God, Njambi, why have you never told me this?'

'You never gave me a chance.'

He lit a cigarette, looking first at the boy, then at his mother. 'Why, why on earth did you desert me if you were carrying my child?'

'I told you I don't know which devil got into me; besides, I didn't know then. It was only the fifth week.'

He rose to his feet and went to the large window. He looked in distress through the lace curtain at the street outside, pulling on his cigarette. 'On second thoughts, I'll never forgive you,' he said finally.

That startled her, for she had thought her revelation would bring them closer. She forgot herself, went over to him and clutched his sleeve. 'You've got to forgive me and take me back!' she cried desperately, and regretted it instantly, since she had not planned to reveal what she wanted so soon.

He raised his eyebrows in his mild way of showing surprise. 'Haven't we been apart too long, Njambi? No doubt you've met others; so have I. We're almost like strangers.'

'But strangers can get to know one another. Is it so difficult for us to do so again, Mwea?'

'I guess not. But I fear it would be all in vain. Perhaps if we'd met again a few months ago . . . But recently I had another nasty experience which warned me never to get involved again.'

Njambi studied him and realised how crushed and worn out he was. She realised then with dismay just how much in love he had been with the stupid chimpanzee of a girl, and still was.

'I wouldn't hurt you again,' she said with much feeling, unaware that she had lost the power to do so. 'Can't we be friends at least?'

'Of course we can always be that.'

That was something at least; it would give her an opportunity to work on him further. 'Can I have my old job back?'

'There is no vacancy at present, but I could look for one for you in another factory.'

She should have got the message then, but she just didn't want to. He sat down again. He produced a cheque book and filled out a cheque in her favour. 'Buy the boy a shirt or something if you're so hard up.'

She took the cheque and stared at it. It could do far more than buy a shirt. It could pay the rent arrears, and for the electricity which had already been disconnected. 'This is extremely kind of you. Thank you very much indeed.'

He shrugged off her gratitude and drained his glass. He said he had an appointment elsewhere, settled the bill and left. He did not actually have an appointment; he just found the whole situation awkward.

She mistook his gesture, which was one of pity for the child, as encouragement for her to pursue him further. She was sure she would get round him in time. But she was equally sure that she would have no chance at all against that stupid Waithera, if he found out that she was innocent and had been framed. There was always that chance! The very idea terrified Njambi. She had to try to get rid of the girl for good!

8

Perils of Love

Waithera had so much to be grateful for, but she was not happy. It was Monday morning, and she was walking to work after spending the night at the farm with her family. Her mother had been discharged; she was even doing the cooking again. The hospital bill had been cleared. Her brother was happy because he'd been able to buy books and other essentials, ready to leave for college. Even the old man could not help smiling, for he had already ordered cement, window panes, ceiling boards and other building materials to complete the house. They were all proud of her, for she had not let them down. Even the weather was being kind to her, for storm clouds were gathering, heralding the coming of the long rains, which would boost production.

Yet Waithera was not happy. She did not care so much what the world thought about her, but Mwea's unjust accusations hurt her deeply.

She'd learned some of the ugly details of what had happened that night, and she couldn't really blame him for thinking she had been drunk. But he should not have been so ready to condemn her. It was all so unfair! If only she had not sat down with the brute who had drugged her!

Then she turned her head and saw the same brute. He was following her, a hundred or so metres behind. He was wearing a hat over his half-bald head, but there was no mistaking his stout figure. She was terrified. She looked around and saw one or two other pedestrians and felt a bit more secure, but she quickened her pace. She would make a run for it and scream if he pursued her, but he did not quicken his pace. Nevertheless she felt he was watching her.

A white Nissan Urvan minibus came humming up the

road. She waved at it frantically, and it stopped. She scrambled in, sighing with relief. She was breathless and agitated as she burst into Mwea's office.

'Please, Mwea, I need . . .' She was stopped short by his expression, which was uncaring with just a touch of mild curiosity.

She did not know that the sight of her gave a twist of the knife with which she had pierced his heart. Her brown, oval face, framed by smoothed hair, was more beautiful than ever. Mwea had forgotten just how pure she looked. How could a cheap, dirty mind be in such a body?

'You need what, Waithera?' he asked.

'Protection. I saw the beast again – the one who drugged me. He was following me on my way here.'

'You mean you didn't sleep here?'

She detected the sneer and bit her lip. 'No, I didn't. I slept in my parents' house, where I could get the warmth I'm lacking here. But on the way I saw the man and I suspect he was following me. I want you to tell him to leave me alone and to protect me from him.'

'And how am I to warn him since I don't know him?'

'You do! He said you do business with him! It was you who told him to expect me at the bar.'

'Then he was lying, or you are. It is obvious you were with him again last night, and as he escorted you here this morning, people saw you and you rushed in here with this movie type of tale of being followed.'

She stared at him in speechless agony. Her eyes glistened with tears. 'I came for protection, and you give me insults?' she sobbed. 'Thank you, Mwea.' She turned and left his office.

For a moment he wondered if he had not wronged her, then he remembered the sight of her in the arms of that ape, and he shrugged off her tears and beauty savagely.

Waithera did not venture out of the factory for two days. She dreaded the thought of going out and meeting the beast again. She recalled his features and eyes vividly and decided he was dangerous. It was too wet to go out anyhow, for the long rains had started with a vengeance. Leaf collection was impossible in some places except by tractor. On the third day the sky cleared somewhat and the sun shone, and she had to go out and inspect a few centres where the leaves had not been collected.

Since Mwea had been unco-operative, she would have to see to her own security. She would make sure that she was never alone. For a while she considered assigning a tough young man to do the rounds with her, but since it was likely to provoke some nasty comment from Mwea, she discarded the idea. Her elderly driver would have to do. He was strong after all. She told him of her fears and asked him to arm himself. He was to look out for the stout, half-bald man, and have him arrested on sight. She was definitely going to press charges against him for having drugged and handled her in an indecent manner.

They visited two centres without incident. The leaves were OK for they had only stayed overnight in a cool temperature. But at the third centre, which was in the remote upper zone, the leaves had not been collected for two days. The centre was on top of a high hill, up a narrow, winding road. They parked the Land Rover facing downhill and approached the block where the farmers were waiting anxiously. Waithera looked around anxiously.

'I'm sorry, we can't buy these. They are spoilt.'

'Are we to blame?' an old man asked bitterly.

'Of course not,' Waithera replied with sympathy. 'But you can't blame us either; our lorries couldn't make it. We can't blame the rain; it's an act of God.'

'KTDA is to blame!' yelled a ragged young man, coming forward. 'Our work is to pick and deliver the leaves on time, which we did. Your work is to collect on time, which you failed to do. It is you who should absorb the losses.'

'I said you can't blame anyone. The whole thing is just unfortunate.'

'Unfortunate, indeed!' yelled the young man, spitting on the ground. 'You tell us to throw away so much labour, and that is all you can say! We demand justice! We demand compensation!'

Most men, the young especially, did not usually take that kind of tone with her, and she looked at him in dislike. He looked familiar. 'I'm sorry; we'll just try our level best to make sure this doesn't happen again.'

'We don't need your apologies. We want to be paid!'

Waithera became angry. 'Then why don't you just take your leaves away, dry them, grind them and sell them wherever you like?'

While they were quarrelling and all attention was on them, the stout, half-bald man appeared from a bush on the opposite side of the road and crept to the Land Rover with a small spanner in his hand.

The ragged young man glared at Waithera, trembling in fury. 'Are you trying to insult me?'

'Who has time to be polite to people like you?' She turned her back on him and spoke to the others. 'You can't blame the . . .'

'Look here, woman . . .'

'Another word to the lady, you rogue,' Waithera's driver said quietly but menacingly, gripping a swordstick he had brought along, 'and I'll thrash you until you're senseless.'

'You can't blame the KTDA, as I was saying. You know it was doing a noble job of tarmacking the roads before the government decided to get paid to do the job. I'll personally plead for a tractor for this location.'

That pacified everyone except the young man. He scowled but said nothing more. She threw him a furious look and made for the Land Rover with her driver. They got in and slammed the doors shut. The man started the engine and the vehicle moved down the hill.

'I've seen that hooligan somewhere,' said Waithera.

'Probably picking pockets,' the driver said in disgust. 'I felt like flogging him.'

'Now where did I see him?' Waithera wondered as the vehicle gathered speed down the hill.

Then she remembered: he was the cyclist who had told her to go to the Muturi bar where she had been drugged! He had been dressed like a factory worker then, but now he had been disguised as a peasant farmer. 'Stop!' she yelled. 'I want to talk to that young man again!'

The driver stepped on the brake pedal, but the vehicle kept on speeding. He tried three more times in vain. 'I can't stop!' he cried in panic. 'We have no brakes!'

'No brakes?' Waithera cried blankly, refusing to believe it since the earthen road down which they were speeding was narrow, rough, steep and winding. 'No brakes?' she repeated in dismay.

'None at all!' he yelled. 'Hang on and pray.'

He switched off the engine, but it did not help for the hill was too steep. The grey Land Rover swerved round one bend like a rocket, hit a pothole which lifted them off their seats, and blundered on to the next bend. Waithera screamed, but the driver controlled his terror and thought swiftly. He could try scraping along the bank to halt the vehicle, but their speed was too fast. Or he could try to stay on the road and risk death in the valley below if he lost control. He kept on the road. Faster and faster rolled the Land Rover. He tried to tame it with gears and failed. He managed to guide it round the second bend, but when they narrowly missed taking off into the air after the third one, he knew he couldn't make it.

'Save yourself!' he yelled as the vehicle half flew round the final bend towards the river below. He abandoned the steering wheel to open his door and Waithera opened hers as the vehicle went bouncing and shooting towards the old, narrow bridge. They both jumped as it smashed into the flimsy side railings and took off into the air. As the two people splashed into the swollen river the vehicle flew over it, landed on the opposite side with an earth-shaking impact, bounced onward, rolling over twice before coming to rest, totally wrecked.

Waithera found herself under the water, unable to see, breathe or scream. Her head broke the surface and she saw to her horror that she was being carried swiftly away by the savage current of the swollen river. She tried to scream but went under again. Her terror made her swallow a lot of water. As she surfaced again she tried to scream as before, but down she went yet again, to swallow more water. The roaring river carried her farther and farther downstream. As she came up for the third time she saw a stout, wooden frame broken from the old bridge. Frantically she clutched it and clung to it, just managing to keep her head above water.The merciless current carried her on and on towards a high, rocky waterfall. She was blinded and deafened by the foaming water as she went over the top. She clung to the timber and survived the fall, but the current retained its fury. It carried her on, smashing her head on a rock. Her world exploded into unconsciousness, and she was carried on, totally at the mercy of the current.

Mwea was basking in the sun, watching a huge, twenty-two-wheel tanker which had delivered petrol to the factory when the news reached him. A clerk came running out from the office block.

'Terrible radio message, sir. KYX has overturned at Karima bridge. Driver's injured. Miss Wagema is missing, feared drowned. A search is required immediately.'

Mwea looked paralysed, as if he'd been struck by extra high voltage. 'What?' he gasped at last. He ran to his car. 'Send a team and call the police!' he yelled as the Pajero roared up the drive and headed for the upper zone like a missile.

A crowd was gathered at the scene. Some people were on the damaged bridge and others were around the wrecked Land Rover, where the driver was seated. His forehead, which was bleeding, was being dressed. The Pajero screeched to a halt and Mwea brushed people aside and stood over him.

'Where is she?' he hissed bitterly. 'Tell me before I kill you!'

'I'm not to blame, sir!' the driver protested. 'The brakes failed just after we started down the hill. She had been afraid of somebody since this morning, and I carried a sword to protect her, but I didn't expect this!'

'What . . . ?' Mwea gasped, remembering Waithera had asked for protection, and he had ignored her. He was to blame. 'Where is she?' he repeated.

'We both jumped. I fell on the bank but she fell into the river.'

Mwea ran to the river, where some of the people were searching already. But when he saw the strength of the current, he raced downriver. If she was dead when he could have protected her, he would never be able to live with himself. Part of him would die with her.

He found her wedged on rocks half a kilometre down, but the current was trying to dislodge her and carry her farther on. Stepping on the rocks, he waded in and dragged her out. He studied her; a sick feeling choked him and dimmed his sight, for she looked more dead than alive. She didn't seem to be breathing, and the back of her head was cut and bloodied.

Mwea controlled his agony and tried to remember some

things about first aid. He pressed her stomach and much water gushed out of her mouth. Swiftly he stripped her of her wet dress. Then he placed his mouth on her nose, took her wrists and started swinging her arms rhythmically, praying, while the sun warmed her. He paused to feel her pulse after a while. It was beating faintly, or was it his imagination? As other people approached he covered her with his jacket, went on working on her as they waited, knowing it was too risky to move her.

He gave a sigh of relief and thanksgiving when, eight minutes later, he was sure she was breathing faintly. There was hope.

Njambi was uneasy that evening. She moved around her flat restlessly. She had unleashed a professional thug on her rival. She was sure that the girl stood no chance, and would be eliminated. But she wondered if what she'd done was not too extreme.

Njambi justified herself by telling herself she had tried other means and failed. Mwea was hers and Waithera had no right to snatch him from her. She deserved to die. And yet Njambi dreaded getting the message she was waiting from the killer – that the deed was done.

She jumped as the phone rang. It was Penina, and she sounded agitated. 'Njambi! Waithera has had an accident!'

'Is she . . . ?' Njambi asked nervously.

'I don't know! She was rushed to a hospital. I called to ask if you had anything to do with it.'

'How could I when I'm a hundred kilometres away?' Njambi asked sharply, since she had not confided in Penina, who could not be trusted with some secrets. 'How did Mwea react?'

'Go and ask him!' Penina yelled. 'I don't want to get involved. When I helped you play pranks, I never thought you'd resort to murder. It isn't amusing! Keep away from me in future or else I'll tell.'

Njambi was shocked and frightened. 'Shut up, you little hyena! This is a public line. You can't tell on me; you're already involved!'

'Keep away from me, you witch!' Penina screamed, and hung up, leaving Njambi more frightened.

———— ♥ ————

Slowly, Waithera became aware she was in a white room with a peculiar smell. She was tucked up in a bed with white sheets, near which was a machine and a shelf. There was also a girl of her own age who was in white. She was seated, knitting. The room was quiet and brightly lit, for it was night time. Waithera was puzzled at first, but she soon realised she was in a ward.

The girl became aware that Waithera was watching her. She put her knitting aside, stood up, bent over her and felt her cheek with the back of her hand. 'Hello, Waithera. I'm your nurse. Can you hear me? You can? Thank heavens you're conscious at last. How do you feel?'

'Numb,' Waithera whispered. 'Headache.'

The nurse nodded. 'You had a bit of a knock on the head.' She did not tell Waithera that she had been brought from ICU, where she had been on oxygen while being treated for shock and concussion. 'But you'll be OK after a bit of rest. So don't try to talk or even think. Try to sleep.'

Waithera could not sleep, for she could not help recalling the horror of all she had undergone. She wondered how she was still alive.

She had to keep guessing until the second day, when she was allowed visitors. The first were her parents, who were utterly relieved to find she was all right, except for weakness and a wound at the back of her head. 'How are you, Mammi? We can't stay away from trouble, you and I.'

'I was nearly brought back here when I heard the news,' said the old lady, unwrapping food she had brought. Then she proceeded to lead them in prayers of thanksgiving to God for sparing her daughter. They then told her how Mwea had rescued her, bought her to the hospital and then gone to the farm to inform them. He had comforted them, and it was he who had brought them here.

Waithera was touched. She had not expected so much concern for her after his indifference and contempt. 'You mean he is here?'

'Yes, and he wishes to see you.'

After the parents had left the man came in. For once he was immaculately dressed in a dark suit with a white shirt and a tie. He was holding a fresh, pink rose, which he had probably picked outside. He gave it to her and smiled. 'Hello, my dear. You had me frightened.'

She looked up at his fine figure and smiled sadly. 'Did you really, really care, Mwea?'

He sat on the edge of her bed and took her hand lightly in his, studying her well-modelled features. 'Yes I did care; I didn't realise how much until I nearly lost you.'

'Did you really?' she asked with a touch of bitterness. 'Yet you refused to protect me.'

Her bluntness startled him. 'That was because of circumstances. If I overreacted, it was because of the intensity of my feelings. Any pain I may have inflicted on you was because of the agony and jealousy of love.'

'Please don't let us talk of love. You mistrust me even more than I do you.'

'There is nothing I crave for more than to feel I can trust you, Waithera, and I know you want to feel the same about me. What has happened has made me suspect I've misunderstood you just as you may have misunderstood me. We haven't been communicating well. Let's do so now before we destroy ourselves. First tell me exactly what happened that night in the bar.'

'I tried to tell you and you didn't listen,' she said resentfully. 'I was looking forward to meeting you at the factory before going out for our date, but a young man with a bicycle and uniform came and told me you had sent him to tell me to meet you at the bar. I met that balding brute instead. He told me that he was waiting for you also, to sell you stock or plots. He persuaded me to take a soda while we waited for you, and I accepted since he claimed you'd pay. I passed out and I didn't know what happened until – but why am I telling you all this since you still won't believe me?'

'I believe you,' he said quietly. 'If I hadn't been so mad about seeing him holding you then, I would have noticed that his hoarse voice was the same one which had called me that morning, telling me to go to the bar where I'd find you drinking.'

Waithera was amazed. 'He did?'

'Yes. It's obvious now that we were both tricked.'

'They tricked me again,' Waithera told him. 'The same young man started a quarrel with me at Karima Centre. I didn't recognise him then because he was disguised as a farm worker. The brute must have tampered with the Land Rover while we were quarrelling. It had been OK before then.'

'He loosened one of the brake pipes, spilling all the fluid at the top of the hill.'

Waithera was horrified. 'Why would they want to kill me?'

Mwea cupped her chin in his hands. 'Help me to help you. Tell me if you know anyone who would want you dead. A rival in inheritance? A jealous boyfriend or even wife?'

'Are you suggesting I have had an affair with a married man?' she asked coldly, removing his hands from her face.

'I'm not overlooking anything! The matter is too serious. Even the police are suspicious, but I want to know more before handing it over to them.'

'Then let me assure you that I have no jealous boyfriend or wife after my blood. It is your girlfriends who are more likely to harm me. Maybe you're still supporting one of them. After all, who would gain from my departure?'

'Who indeed?' he repeated, staring at her, his mind racing. 'It is all beginning to make sense.'

'What is?'

'We'll discuss it soon, but I'll have to be busy first.' He bent and kissed her forehead. 'Get well in the meantime.'

He left, leaving her wondering what he was going to do.

9

Two-timing Love

Waithera was discharged from the hospital after a week, but told to take it easy for the rest of the month. So she stayed at home, just cooking and cleaning when she was not relaxing with her favourite hobbies, which were feature movies, novels and embroidery. They helped to pass the time while her shattered nerves recovered.

But she was still nervous in a way: she still did not know who her enemies were, and whether they would strike again. Mwea had assured her that he would take care of the matter. She was guarded night and day by two men with a fierce dog.

Mwea became more kind and considerate to her than ever before, so much so that she almost forgot how nasty he had been to her. He never went home without dropping in to see how she was getting on, bringing her video cassettes, novels or refreshments like Lucozade. Penina the snooper, like the rest of the factory, decided that Emma Waithera was certainly back in favour. Even Mboche, the factory Casanova, sadly postponed his plans for buying Waithera beer, as he could not afford a new set of teeth if the boss caught him at it.

Since Waithera was not allowed outside her home, she longed for company sometimes, when Mwea or her mother were not there. She tried to call Mama Asha twice and failed to reach her. But she was pleased to hear her friend call one evening.

'I tried to ring you twice last week, Waithera. I've been worried about you. I feared you had quit. Where have you been?'

'In hospital.' Waithera proceeded to tell her friend what had happened, though she did not say it had been sabotage, as Mwea had forbidden her to do so in case the culprits were alerted. Mama Asha was horrified.

'What an awful thing to have happened! No wonder I was so worried about you. But Allah is all merciful, since you're able to talk to me now.'

'Yes, it was His mercy which guided Mwea to me, to give me first aid before my life flickered out. The doctor told me I wouldn't have survived if he hadn't done so.'

There was a pause. 'How are you two getting along?'

'We had a nasty misunderstanding, but we made it up after the accident. He appears to be more fond of me than ever, but I'm scared at the thought of giving in, for he would then be bored with me.'

There was another pause. 'Perhaps I wronged him by warning you against him, Waithera dear. His actions have proved his good intentions.' Mama Asha paused. 'You say he saved your life. Well, you owe him more. It was he who furnished your house and enabled your father to get the loan.'

Waithera gasped and felt faint. She put the receiver down and covered her face with her hands. She was not stupid. She had suspected something of the kind all along, and now that her friend had confirmed it, his marvellous kindness could not help but move her. What overcame her even more was the fact that he had done it without her knowledge and without putting her under any obligation to him. He had not even claimed to have saved her life; it was the doctor who had told her. He was not vain and self glorifying, but noble. The kind of man she wanted, except for one thing . . .

She picked up the receiver. Mama Asha was calling her. 'Hello! Waithera! Are you still there?'

'I am. You're my friend Mama Asha, and you meant well. I'm overcome with gratitude . . . even love . . . for him. But you placed me in the snare I wanted to avoid, for I haven't made up my mind, since I am still worried by his past behaviour.'

'None of us is perfect, Waithera; even you aren't. You can be stubborn and you don't speak your mind sometimes. I don't know what it takes to convince you, but you have to make a choice now before you reach the point of no return.'

Njambi entered the restaurant hesitantly. A month has passed since the car crash, but she was still uneasy. She was not sure what was going on at the factory, since Penina had firmly broken their ties. All Njambi knew was that Waithera had survived. Had the girl got him back through sympathy, or had she been crippled and disfigured, becoming less attractive? Njambi hoped so! But had foul play been suspected? She hoped not.

It was her curiosity which had brought her there now, to find Mwea and learn what she could from his attitude. If he was still crazy about the stupid Waithera, then she would leave them alone. But no! Why should she? Just because the girl was younger and prettier? It took far more than pretty faces to hold men, and she, Njambi, was more experienced. 'I'll see how far she'll go with her silly schoolgirl airs!' she decided.

She sat down and a waiter who was watching her came over. 'Excuse me, Madam, but aren't you the one who was with Mr Mwea sometime back?'

'That's likely. Why do you ask?'

'He told me to ask you to call him at the office or at home.' He produced a piece of paper. 'These are the numbers.'

Njambi was excited. Mwea wanted to see her! Perhaps he wanted closer ties because of his son. She could hardly wait for evening to come so she could call him at home, wherever it was.

But as she made the call she was uneasy, and wondered if

he had connected her in any way with Waithera's accident. However, she was reassured when his low voice came on the line, for it sounded pleased. 'I was afraid you had disappeared again.'

'I've been busy Mwea, but of course not too busy to remember . . . er . . . old friends.'

'Yes. You said we could get acquainted again, Njambi. I was wondering if we could not meet again soon?'

'Why not?' Njambi said casually, suppressing her excitement. 'When do you suggest?'

'The day after tomorrow, same place, four o'clock sharp. Can you make it?'

'I'll try.'

'Don't fail, Black Beauty. I've missed you.'

He hung up, leaving her more excited than ever, for that was the pet name he'd once called her.

———— ♥ ————

Waithera studied herself in the wardrobe mirror and decided she was all right. The clear eyes staring back at her from an almost glowing complexion declared she was as healthy as she could get. The delicate waves of hair crowning the oval face were not so bad either. But she was not so sure whether her light green dress was OK. It was tight at the top and pleated at the bottom. Over the round collar were her flame coloured beads, and hugging her slim waist was her broad, black belt. She wanted to look her best, for Mwea had formally asked her for a date at last, and she had accepted. But even if she was eager, the eyes staring back at her in the mirror told her that she was tense at the same time.

The way he had looked at her suggested that something was going to happen. She was not so sure whether she wanted any such thing yet. Part of her was with him but there was still the remainder which rebelled. She just hadn't made up her mind how to react if he resumed his assault on her. All she was sure of was that she wouldn't want to tread where she was not absolutely sure. Many a girl had come to grief by making a false step.

She applied mildly perfumed lotion to her face and hands and turned away from the mirror. She went to the sitting room, where she tried to relax with a glass of hot cocoa and a romance on the video.

Mwea came in presently with his jacket hung over his arm. He paused to drink in her gleaming simplicity. She looked new every time he met her. 'Good afternoon, dear. I need not ask how you are. You're looking fine.'

'I'm afraid you look tired yourself,' she said, rising to take his jacket and hang it up. 'Let me get you a basin of hot water and some refreshment.'

After he had washed his face and arms, combed his hair and taken a glass of hot cocoa with her, he looked more relaxed. 'It's been quite a busy day,' he told her. 'I'm glad to tell you that since the rains started, production has been rising steadily. Soon it will be above capacity. All high grades, thanks to you.'

'I'm glad my efforts are appreciated,' she murmured in delight.

'Indispensible, pretty girl. I'm glad I backed you. You're to resume work with effect from Monday. Your assistant doesn't quite have your drive. But there's time enough to discuss business. There is much more for you to learn today. Are you ready for our outing?'

'I am,' she murmured shyly, and rose to get a sweater and handbag.

When she returned she found him talking on the phone in a way which suddenly shattered her gay mood and made her sick. How dared he do it in her own house! Did he take her as lightly as she had always suspected?

'. . . so glad to hear you're already there for our date,' he was saying, 'but I'm afraid I got held up. Business matters. I can't make it for two hours or so. Can you wait there in the meantime? Order anything you like . . . Yes, two hours . . . You'll wait? There's a good girl. See you.'

Waithera felt faint and leaned against the wall. 'Who – who was that?'

'Just an old friend who wants to marry me,' he answered casually, watching her closely.

The unbelieving Waithera felt more faint. 'Then – then why don't you go to her? Why bother with me?'

'I said she wants me; I didn't say I wanted her. Anyhow, why should you care if I encourage another, Emma Waithera?' he asked with a touch of bitterness. 'Ever since I met you, you've always recoiled from my advances. You've told me time and again to leave you alone. You don't care for me at all.'

His words stung her. 'Th-that isn't true!' she protested. 'I only wanted you to prove your love.' She felt her eyes getting wet and she covered them. 'B-but now, just when I was beginning t-t-to have faith in you, you've ruined everything. So call your woman and tell her you're free to join her after all. I'll never be one of your casuals.'

He watched her with interest. 'When you finish saying your piece, Waithera, we'll get moving. There's much for you to learn today, as I said.'

Njambi stood looking down at the telephone in irritation. She had been looking forward to meeting and captivating Mwea, and now he said he would be held up for two hours. There was nothing else for her to do but wait.

She moved in her graceful manner across the restaurant to a table near one of the large windows with lace curtains. Her face was carefully made up to look younger and more beautiful. She was wearing well-patterned hair pieces with falls. In her earlobes were jewels, while she wore a neat jacket over a flowered dress with slits at the sides. She sat down and ordered brandy. Then she remembered she was supposed to be religious and ordered lemonade instead. She sat sipping and watching the street through the transparent curtains.

She saw a young man with a new one-ton pick-up park and enter the place. He looked around and his eyes lit up with interest as they rested on her. He came over to her table and sat down. Njambi looked him over and thought he seemed fine and prosperous enough, but since she was expecting Mwea she was not at all keen on him.

He ordered a drink and scrambled eggs and then grinned at her. 'Hi. After the rains it is too beautiful a day for you to be so glum.'

'I'm fine, thank you.'

'I can tell you're feeling dejected. That's not right for a person as beautiful as yourself. You're probably waiting for somebody. An ungrateful fellow, not to appreciate his good fortune. He should be the one who is waiting.'

'Shut up and mind your own business.'

He did not seem to mind. 'Sorry, no offence meant. It's just that I can't understand why some fellow would keep such a beauty waiting when I could offer a fortune for the privilege.'

As he took his snack he kept on talking and she soon gathered he was a rancher from the area. He often came to town to supply produce or to buy materials. She was still not interested, but when the time came for him to settle the bill, he produced a fat pile of notes from the inside pocket of his coat. Since they were all of large amounts he checked the other pocket and pulled out an even bigger wad of the same kind of notes. Finally he found the lesser notes in his rear pocket, and he gave one of them to the waiter, telling him to keep the change. Njambi could not help staring and quivering. The fellow was a mobile bank!

'Are you sure you won't take a drink with me?' he asked as he rose to leave.

'Another time, thank you,' she answered more politely.

'Are you afraid of your date? He isn't worth it. Why not come with me to a better place? I'll make it worth your while.'

Njambi was tempted, but she was expecting Mwea. 'My tastes are expensive,' she heard herself say.

'So are mine.'

Njambi thought it over and decided since she was desperate for money, she would be stupid not to clean up the fool. She could always meet Mwea another day and claim she'd got tired of waiting. 'OK, let's go, but not near here.'

He was overjoyed. 'You'll like it at the ranch.'

Njambi told him to wait for her up the street, in case Mwea appeared unexpectedly, or be told by a waiter when he did turn up. When she was in the pick-up, they made for the vast plains beyond, which were entirely flat except for the huge mountain towering above. The region was suitable for dairy farming, and there were such farms all over.

Njambi and her new admirer got to know one another. He was called Nderi, was thirty-three years old, and he lived on the slopes of the mountain. Njambi was afraid the place would bore her. But when he stopped the pick-up before it, she gasped in awe and admiration. He led her to the fence for a better view. It was actually an estate, a few kilometres square. There was a private drive passing through green fields with many herds of cattle, some of which were as huge as buffaloes. Beyond were vast fields of wheat. In the middle of the estate was a beautiful, one-storey mansion with a red tile roof surrounded by park-like grounds. In the background was the blue mountain with its snow-covered peaks.

'Would you like to live here?'

'Who wouldn't?' she replied, looking at him in a new light. She had not known he was a millionaire. 'It must be flowing with milk and wheat.'

'Yes, but I like it most because it's beautiful and peaceful, far from the noise and pollution of towns. It can even make you live longer.'

'It must be nice to live in a place of plenty when there's so much hunger around.'

'It was not always so,' he said, putting an arm round her slender waist. 'It took years of hard work to develop. Note how recent the main house is.'

She slipped her arm around him also. 'Yes, it must have taken a lot of hard work and dedication.'

A white Pajero with orange stripes pulled up behind their pick-up, and Njambi shuddered in dismay. She hastily pulled her arm from round Nderi. It was Mwea! He was with the stupid Waithera; he spoke to her and they both got out of the car. They walked towards Njambi and her boyfriend, who looked relaxed as before. As for Waithera, she looked bewildered. Mwea was grim and menacing. The situation confused and scared Njambi. What did it all mean?

10

Moment of Truth

'Mwea! Wh-what are you doing here?' Njambi gasped when she finally found her voice.

'*You* tell me first what you're doing,' he hissed in contempt. 'I thought we had a date elsewhere? I thought you said you had reformed – that you'd never let me down again?'

'I – I never would,' Njambi said desperately. 'I got tired of waiting for you, and since it was getting late this man offered to take me to his wife, who is a sister in Christ.'

Mwea laughed mirthlessly. 'She won't be so sisterly if she sees you holding him like that.'

That sunk Njambi. 'Now you tell me what you're doing here with this woman if you're holier.'

'I came to meet you, Njambi. You see, I'm not so surprised to see you.'

'What do you mean?' she asked uneasily.

'It means you've been had.' Mwea turned to the other man, who was still relaxed. 'Did you have much trouble persuading her to come?'

'No, sir,' Nderi replied. 'I just flashed the milk cash at her as you suggested, and she was ready to follow me to hell itself.'

'Wha-a-t?' Njambi exclaimed in shock. 'You know each other?'

'We ought to,' Nderi told her with as much contempt as Mwea. 'I work for him.'

'You mean . . . ?' Njambi gasped in greater shock, her eyes and mouth wide open as she gaped first at the estate, then at Mwea.

'Yes, he owns it. I never said I did, did I? I only said I lived there. I manage it.'

'And he has done a damn good job of it,' Mwea said, 'just as he managed to bring you here.'

He looked at his watch. It was nearly six. 'Milk delivery is late, Nderi. Those who were milking must be waiting. Why don't you go down with the pick-up and tend to the matter while I tend to this one?'

'Certainly, Mr Mwea.' He hurried to the pick-up and drove up the private drive, watched by a stunned Njambi.

Waithera was also stunned. She had been sulking on their way here after learning Mwea was two-timing her, and the revelations which had begun to unfold astonished her.

Mwea turned to her. 'Have you met this mama?' he asked her, gesturing towards the more slender, taller and more sophisticated Njambi.

'Yes,' Waithera answered, looking elsewhere, as if she did not want to remember.

'Where?'

'When I was with you at the hotel.'

'Did you meet her again after that?'

'Yes.'

'Where? When?'

Waithera paused, as if she was finding the questions distasteful. 'At my place, after you and I had lunch together. She used my phone.'

'What did she tell you?'

Waithera ran her gleaming black shoe over the grass and said nothing.

'Don't be tiresome! Tell me what happened.'

Waithera want on running her shoe over the grass. Then she looked up at him sulkily. 'She showed me your son. You dropped her when she conceived.'

'I suspected as much,' Mwea muttered grimly. 'It was around that time you distanced yourself from me. When I asked you why, you said it was because of something you had seen – something I had not confessed. You thought I was a monster and have recoiled from me ever since. I didn't understand because I didn't know the boy existed then; only recently she showed him to me for the first time. I brought you here today to learn the truth of the matter. There is much for you to know as I told you.

'Njambi was my first love whom I told you about from the start when we were fishing. I said she deserted me for material wealth and nearly wrecked my life. To you she claimed it was I who deserted her. To prove I was speaking the truth I decided to demonstrate it in this somewhat dramatic way. I made a date with her and deliberately let you, Waithera, hear me making it over the phone, knowing all the time I'd show you how easily she could run away with another. Or do you still believe her?'

Waithera shook her head.

Mwea turned to Njambi, who was not only thoroughly ashamed but afraid. 'You almost had me fooled by your religion story, but not quite. Leopards don't change their spots, do they? You're going to confess *everything* from the start to the finish, and apologise to Waithera.'

'Why should I?' Njambi asked defiantly, though she sounded more frightened than anything.

'Because if you don't, I'll have you locked up and charged with attempted murder.'

There was a pause in which Njambi quivered with terror while Waithera was horrified. The only sound was that of vehicles which kept roaring past at high speed. 'Murder?' Waithera gasped. 'Whose murder?'

'Yours, of course,' Mwea told her. 'Remember how we wondered who could have gained from your elimination? You put me on the track by suggesting it was one of my women. I recalled Njambi here had recently asked me to take her back, and I suspected her. My suspicion was confirmed after investigations. After you were nearly drowned, I remembered bitterly that I had refused to listen to you when you said your life was in danger. I was sure then that you had spoken the truth when you claimed that you had been drugged at the bar. I went there and discovered that you, Njambi, had been with the thug who drugged Waithera. You were helped by your nosey friend Penina, who is due to be sacked. It must have been you who hatched the plan. A wicked trick, though I must admit it was a masterstroke; to discredit Waithera before my eyes. You had her lured to the trap, and made sure I arrived there at the right time. It worked and I was made at you, Waithera.

'But when Njambi met me she must have known my heart was still with you, so she decided to send her thug to finish you off. That was why he was following you around, until he found a suitable opportunity of sabotaging your vehicle.'

Njambi recoiled from Waithera's horror more than she did from Mwea's anger. 'You . . . ?' gasped the girl. 'Why . . . why would you want to kill me? Someone you don't know? I never harmed you! I never told you to keep away from him!'

'I didn't do it!' Njambi said wildly, looking around. She noticed a Hiace minibus speeding towards them and she ran towards the road to stop it.

Mwea rushed after her, gripped her arm and pulled her back towards the fence. 'Not so fast! I said you're going to confess and apologise, or else go to jail. Take your choice.'

'I didn't do it!' Njambi shrieked.

'Get a rope from the boot of the car, Waithera,' Mwea ordered. 'We'll hand her over to those who are experts in persuading people to talk.'

'Please don't, Waithera,' Njambi pleaded, seeing Mwea was serious. 'It's true I had you drugged and tried to have you killed. But I have nothing against you personally. It's just that you stood in my way. I now realise I was stupid and crazy. Please forgive me; I'm sorry.'

Waithera said nothing, but just stared at the woman as if she was a creature from outer space. 'Well, do you accept her apology or not?' Mwea asked. Waithera nodded, but he retained his grip on Njambi's arm.

'You caused me much suffering in the past and I forgave you,' he hissed, 'but I won't forgive the recent agony you've caused with your lies and tricks unless you undo the harm a bit by telling her exactly what happened between us.'

'All right,' Njambi sobbed, breaking down. 'It was I who deserted him. I went away with another when we were about to get married. I – I didn't realise then that I was . . . pregnant. I have regretted it . . . ever since. It was desperation . . . which drove me to extremes. Once again I say I'm sorry to both of you. Now please leave me alone.'

Mwea glared at her, let go of her and took Waithera's hand. He led her to the car, slammed the door shut and started the engine, but he did not engage gear. He stopped to look at the woman they were leaving, weeping alone by the roadside as night approached.

'Sorry I can't invite you in. You once had better places to go than meeting my mother.' He produced several notes and dropped them out of the window. 'You'd better take a bus back to town and book a room. You were once very good, Njambi. I don't know what happened to you. I believe you need psychiatric help. If you do seek it and become as good as you once were, then I might instruct my manager to advance you a loan for your business for the sake of your child.' He engaged gear and drove along the straight drive of the estate.

Njambi watched them go, though her sight was blurred by tears. The fact that the estate might have been hers instead of the stupid Waithera's drove her to the verge of insanity. She even contemplated suicide. But finally she collected herself, picked up the money he had thrown as if it was a bone to a dog, and stopped a passenger pick-up. She squeezed herself in and people looked at her curiously as it roared off.

Though Njambi had been left, she remained on Waithera's mind, and somewhat spoiled the surprises which awaited her. Five hundred metres up the drive, they went through a gate of wrought-iron into the park-like compound of the new, one-storey mansion. It was surrounded by a trimmed hedge, flower gardens and young trees. Nearby was a smaller brick house from colonial days, which probably housed the manager. There was also a row of rooms for the workers. Several men and women were loading milk jars on to the pick-up as Nderi watched, and they stopped to stare at the smart, brown beauty their employer helped out of the Pajero. He led her to the front verandah, where a strong old lady and a younger one of thirty were waiting.

'My mother and my sister Sylvia,' Mwea told her as they shook hands.

'How are you?' said the sister warmly. 'You must be Waithera. We have been expecting you and eager to see you.'

'Yes, for Mwea has never brought us someone to dine with us,' said the old lady, scrutinising the girl. She approved of the innocent face, but was suspicious of the smart, light-green dress with the gleaming black belt and shoes.

'Don't be unnerved by Mother,' Mwea said, smiling. 'She is wondering if you can toil on the land, when you've done so all your life. She is actually most friendly and considerate, just as you are. I'm sure you'll all like one another.'

The mother smiled as well. 'I'm sure we shall. Come in and welcome, Waithera. Sylvia will get you something to drink while I make supper, after which we'll talk.'

This bewildered Waithera. She was ushered into a small hall of a sitting room, which was designed like the set of a movie. It awed and almost frightened her, since she was used to living simply. Presently the sister helped them wash their hands before serving them with hot milk.

'So you're Waithera. It's so nice to have you with us. Now perhaps Mwea will recover his appetite.'

'He has been talking about me?'

'Only to me. I'll tell you all about it sometime.' She winked. 'I'm going to help Mama with the cooking. Feel at home in the meantime.'

Waithera sipped her milk, avoiding looking at Mwea. 'You – you didn't inform me I was going to meet your mother.'

'I had to. You're the type a fellow wouldn't mind taking home to Mother. Do you mind?'

'Not really, but I was so – unprepared. By the way, where is your father?'

'He keeps a shop elsewhere, but he comes occasionally.' He rose to his feet. 'Come.'

He led her past several rooms to the rear verandah. Beyond were the vast fields of wheat, with the majestic mountain towering in the background. Its snow-covered peaks were bathed in various colours by the setting sun. A chilly breeze rustled the wheat.

'It's so beautiful but cold here,' Waithera said, then added; 'I didn't know you were so rich.'

'Not really. I have many burdens. But with luck and harder work, I'll make it. This place was originally owned by a white settler, who sold it to a politician. The latter mismanaged it and sold it to me, and it's now succeeding. But there's something more precious to me than all this. Do you realise why I want you to know Mother?'

'Yes,' she whispered.

He noticed she was shivering, and he removed his jacket and placed it on her shoulders. 'Don't feel I'm forcing you. You can still back out. But you've got to know that I've grown to love you more and more ever since I first saw you. Even through the most trying period, I've tried hard to be worthy of your trust. Say you do, and fill me with matchless joy, as only you, my angel Emma Waithera can.'

She looked up at him. 'I trust you completely. I was stupid to believe that horrid creature rather than you.'

He grinned in joy as he opened his arms. 'Then why are you standing there, shivering?' She stepped into them shyly, and they closed around her. She sighed at the feel of his warmth and strength, while he shuddered with excitement at the feel of her soft, healthy and mildly perfumed curves against him. 'Or don't you feel you can return my love a little?'

'I – I have grown to love you also,' she murmured. 'I realised it when that nasty woman showed me the boy, for I was upset. I was even more upset when you were angry with me and you ignored me after the bar incident. But what convinced me was your kindness by helping me with furniture and the loan, among other things, like your concern for my mother.'

'How did you find out about the furniture and loan?'

'Mama Asha told me after she thought I was being unfair to you. But in spite of wanting you I was afraid of giving in in case you discarded me as Njambi claimed you would. But now that I know she was lying I'm not afraid to confess that I – that I love you too.'

The words are so common, and yet from her lips they sounded miraculous. He could hardly believe it. Nor could he believe it when she arched her body against his when he hugged her closer, and tilted her head back to receive his kiss without her usual resistance. Their world burst into something which was beautiful and exciting beyond comparison.

'Say that again,' he muttered.

But lights came on all over the house and grounds, breaking the magic. Mwea took her back to the sitting room of her future home.

CHELSEA HOUSE HEARTBEATS

The book you have been reading is part of the new Chelsea House Heartbeats series. Details of some of the other titles available are listed below.

A Bride for the King
NANDI DLOVU

Beautiful Zible dearly loves Saul. Then the royal *sangoma* declares the Zible will marry Saul's half-brother – the king. The young lovers are heart-broken. Against a background of sorcery and intrigue, Zible prepares to meet her fate . . .

Stolen Kisses
MICHELLE MWANSA

Shy schoolgirl Patience meets young lawyer Artwell Nkosi in the library. She is swept off her feet. Is this true love, or is Artwell really after her sister, the glamorous model Thandiwe?

The Gift of Life
PATRICIA CAGE

When Thembi wins the heart of Mduduzi, everyone agrees that this is a match made in heaven. Suddenly, at their engagement party, disaster strikes. Will things ever be the same again?

Please Forgive Me

ROSINA UMELO

Oke and Bukky love each other dearly. But Oke's sister, Udoka, will have nothing to do with the girlfriend she calls a witch. Oke and Udoka are involved in a tragic car accident and suddenly it all looks like Bukky's fault . . .

Heart of Love

HOPE DUBE

Claudette is hard-working and new to the company. She is bright and beautiful. Charles Daka is her boss, and is rich, successful and single. How can Claudette get him to take her seriously and find her attractive?

Love Changes Everything

KALU OKPI

In exile in Nigeria, stylish Gavinah finds love in the arms of Onyeukwu, law student and rock musician. But her tragic past soon catches up with her and it seems that the young lovers will never be together . . .

The Jasmine Candle
CHRISTINE A. BOTCHWAY

Zenobia, a mysterious beauty, lives a lonely life in a land between two ancient tribes. Even her childhood friend Odole doesn't want to know her. Then she breaks a taboo and Odole is ordered to kill her. Our heroine seems doomed.

When the Drum Speak of Love
SHIRLEY BOJÉ

Pretty Lindidwe wants to see a bit of the world before she marries gentle Sipho. She jumps at the chance of a holiday in the city. Behind the bright lights, she discovers the charming Richard Zondi. How can she ever turn back?

The Place of Gentle Waters
JESSICA MAJI

Scientist Anne Caldwell arrives from Britain to go to Richard Giba's Kenyan farm to help him with a problem. She soon finds herself attracted to him. But Anne had a dark secret . . .